ABOUT THE AUTHOR

Michael Coleman was born a couple of hefty goal-kicks away from West Ham United's football ground, which probably doesn't explain why he dreamed of becoming a footballer. In the event he became a computer boffin with both Portsmouth University and IBM, until he discovered that writing books was much more fun.

At school, his favourite subjects were PE, Maths and girls - but not always in that order. The Snog Log is about the sort of competition he and his mates might well have tried if they'd thought of it at the time. He also wanted to put into a story some of the important lessons he's learned since then.

Other Titles by Michael Coleman

Black Apples
Tag
Weirdo's War

Super Crunchies
Angels FC Series

ORCHARD BOOKS
96 Leonard Street, London EC2A 4XD
Orchard Books Australia
Unit 31/56 O'Riordan Street, Alexandria, NSW 2015
ISBN 1 84121 161 3
A PAPERBACK ORIGINAL
First published in Great Britain in 2001
Text © Michael Coleman 2001
The right of Michael Coleman to be identified as the
author of this work has been asserted by him in accordance
with the Copyright, Designs and Patents Act, 1988.
A CIP catalogue record for this book
is available from the British Library.
3 5 7 9 10 8 6 4 2
Printed in Great Britain

MICHAEL COLEMAN

ORCHARD BOOKS

To the class of '57
Barking Abbey Grammar School

Contents

emotion {Latin *emotio -onem*, from *emovere* (to move)} n. Agitation of the mind; a state of excited feeling of any kind, whether of pain or pleasure.

First Week of Term
Studying the Form

Whenever he thought about it – and he did, regularly – Robbie came to the same conclusion. The whole business had really begun with the sudden and totally mesmerising debut of Melanie Bradshaw's bongos. That's where he would have pinned the blame – given half a chance!

Until then the first day back after the summer break had run true to form. Timetable-copying. Pep-talk-hearing. Corridor-tramping. In a word, boring. And, with their sparkly new Mr Carmichael of an English teacher having just turned up, not looking like it was going to improve.

Then Robbie had gazed idly across the room. Hayley McLeod had bent forward to whisper something in Melanie's ear – only for Melanie to answer her, not by turning round, but by leaning blouse-stretchingly backwards...

He'd goggled. He knew he'd goggled. What red-blooded Year 9 wouldn't have? Melanie Bradshaw, Microscopic Mel, the girl with a chest so flat she could use it for geometry whenever she left her set square at home, had finally developed...well, *developed*! That was the only word for it. If the front of Mel's blouse wasn't a good bit nearer the blackboard than last term then it was time he went for an eye test.

Stirred, Robbie shifted his gaze to other parts of the room. Hayley McLeod's legs had grown longer, hadn't they? Either that, or her skirt had shrunk.

Purity Meek had changed her hairstyle, surely? Instead of letting it dangle like spaghetti, she had it held in place with a grip a crocodile could have used as a set of false teeth. Very sophisticated!

As for Zoë Freeman, she'd definitely had her nose pierced. Robbie could see the gold stud. Puffin' hell, what with the four holes along her right ear and one above her left eyebrow, Zoë's head was starting to look like it had got woodworm! The question was, had she had anything else pierced that wasn't visible to the naked eye?

Ultimate test: Sandra 'Amazon' Adams. Had she morphed over the summer into something more like a female and less like a block of flats? Not a chance...

'Gentleman by the window! Are you with this class, or merely visiting?'

As he heard Mr Carmichael's shout, Robbie jerked up straight. Too straight. And too quickly. He heard the sniggers. Not good. He needed a snappy reply.

'With it, Mr Carmichael? Yep, I'm with it all right!' *Not bad. Not bad at all!*

Carmichael smiled, checking a class plan at the same time. 'Are you now, Mr…Brookes? We shall see.'

That was it. No moans about giving him lip. Robbie could have named half a dozen other teachers who'd have screwed him to the wall.

Turning away, Carmichael scanned the room. 'Right, everybody now the proud owner of a new notebook? Then open sesame!'

Robbie looked down. While he'd been sizing up Melanie Bradshaw, a chunky red book had appeared in front of him. He flipped the cover open.

'As you will have already spotted,' Carmichael was saying, 'your notebook is currently note-less. That's bad news and good news. You want the bad news first? Course you do. They're blank because I want you to write in them.'

Ignoring the groans, he turned to the board. 'The good news, however, is that these are the only words I will insist you *do* write in them…'

With one eye on his book and the other on the shifting bulges in Melanie's ice-blue blouse, Robbie copied what Carmichael had written:

'Poetry is the spontaneous overflow of
powerful feelings. It takes its origin from
emotion reflected in tranquillity.'
　　　　William Wordsworth (1770–1850)

'Wordsworth,' said Carmichael when they'd finished.
'Anybody know anything about him?' He looked
Robbie's way. 'How about you, Mr With-it?'

Robbie felt the eyes of the class on him. 'He's dead?'
he shrugged.

It was a deliberately dumb answer, got a laugh like it
was meant to. But again Carmichael didn't let him have
it, just said, 'Most people born in 1770 now are.
Anybody else?'

On the other side of the room a hand went up.
Slowly and blouse-stretchingly. 'He wrote that poem
about daffodils, didn't he?' asked Melanie.

Carmichael nodded, glancing again at the class
plan. 'Quite right, Miss...Bradshaw. Everybody
remember it? "I wandered lonely as a cloud," etc.,
"a host of golden daffodils" etc. A classic poem of
observation.'

He scanned the room once more. 'Which is why I've
paid out of my very own pocket for those notebooks.
Or, more accurately, those *log-books*. Because this term
I want you all to act like Mr Wordsworth and observe

the world. Make notes of what affects your emotions: what excites you, what saddens you. Study places, people, things, each other...'

'How about each other's things, Mr Carmichael?' grinned Robbie.

It was a good one all right. The other lads hooted. Plenty of the girls giggled. Carmichael ignored it – or so he thought.

'And I solemnly promise,' the teacher went on, 'that everything you write in your logs will be for your eyes only. I will never, repeat never, ask to see them.'

That was when he turned Robbie's way. 'Which should answer your question, Mr Brookes,' he smiled. 'That is your log-book. You can write whatever you like in it. Details of people. Details of things. Details of your own thing if you find that of particular interest, Mr Brookes...'

Robbie felt his face going redder than a Manchester United shirt with a nasty dose of sunburn.

You're a pillock, Carmichael! And a total dumbhead. Who do you think's going to bother writing that sort of crud in your puffin' log-books anyway?

Monday 7th September.
'Poetry is the spontaneous overflow of powerful feelings. It takes its origin from

emotion reflected in tranquillity.'

William Wordsworth (1770-1850)

I can't believe I'm writing this! Mel Bradshaw, poetry boff? Hayley and the others would have a fit if they knew!

But that lesson today was different. When Mr Carmichael (rumour has it his first name's Dave) looked at me with those bright blue eyes it was like being picked out by the beam from a lighthouse!

So - here goes with my first two emotional observations:

1. DC's explanations were - what? Mature, that's what they were. All lesson he was trotting out words like emotions and feelings and passions without batting an eyelid. When Mrs Follett used them in that Personal Relationships session last term she got so hot she nearly set off the sprinkler system! And as for the way he skewered Robbie Brookes - classic! (Emotion: admiration.)

2. Compared to him, the boys in our year are so...well, the word's obvious: immature. They're moving backwards. Last year they were almost normal. Now they are sub-normal. At this rate by Year 11 they will be taking GNVQ's in dummy-sucking and potty-training! (Emotion: nausea!)

Robbie's dad speared a sausage, stuck it in his mouth sideways, then aimed his fork across the breakfast table. His hey-I'm-expensive watch had a smudge of tomato sauce on it.

'What d'you learn yesterday then, son? Come on. Gimme a fact.'

'Oh, leave him to eat his breakfast,' sighed Robbie's mum.

'One fact, Julie, that's all I'm after. Not the whole Encyclopiddlier Britannica.'

'It's the way you ask, Vince. You're always so aggressive.'

'That's me, sweetheart. Half tiger, half man. A deadly combination of animal instincts and rippling muscle.'

'Especially between the ears,' muttered Mrs Brookes.

Robbie had seen conversations like this turn into slanging matches too often. His mum wasn't so bad, but his old man – he'd thought of him in that way for so long that in his head he'd given him the initials OM – could start an argument in an empty church. When they started banging on it always made Robbie feel sick to the stomach. That was bad enough at any time, but at eight in the morning...

He dived in quickly, pulling out a fact at random. 'A bloke named Wordsworth,' he said, 'reckoned poetry is all about emotions.'

The OM snorted. 'Oh, very impressive! That will come in handy out in the big, wide world!'

'Leave him alone, Vince,' interrupted Mrs Brookes. 'Just because you didn't do any good at school...'

Another snort, but this time with a wink for Robbie's mum's benefit. 'Weren't interested, was I? Too busy thinking about sowing wild oats, weren't I!'

Mrs Brookes laughed; it was the sort that told Robbie peace had broken out for a while. Just in case, he gulped his breakfast down fast and shot off, saying he'd got to pack his bag for school.

Upstairs he yanked out Carmichael's book and sent it skimming beneath his bed. Make notes about his emotions? He'd sooner sit on an ant-hill with his zip undone! And as for Carmichael never wanting to see what they'd written – what sort of teacher thought like that? A liar, that's what sort. One who was as big a liar as the OM. Wild oats. The bloke had never been near a farm in his life!

Robbie hadn't been the only one girl-spotting the day before. Daz Hogg, built like a small buffalo but not quite as good-looking, had been at it as well. He caught up with Robbie just as he bowled through the school gates.

'Here, Brookesie. Get a look at Hayley McLeod's legs

yesterday did ya?' Daz let his tongue flop out, dog-like.

Robbie grinned. 'Couldn't miss 'em, Daz, not the way she kept hitching that skirt up.'

'Too right!' honked Daz. 'Puffin' hell, I followed her out of English and it was so high I thought I was going to see what she'd had for lunch!'

The mention of English reminded Robbie, as if he'd needed a reminder, of his number-one observation. 'How about Micro Mel, then? Some *outstanding* progress there, I reckon!'

Daz gave a dismissive sniff. 'Sorry. Compared to Chesty's they're just a couple of gnat-bites.'

Robbie knew who – and what – he was picturing. 'Chesty' Weston: PE, History and 42DD minimum! Carmichael might have thought his log-book scheme was all bright and original, but everybody knew that Daz Hogg had been emotionally observing Chesty ever since he'd first seen her demonstrating how to bounce on a trampoline.

'Daz,' grinned Robbie. 'Accept it. You've got no chance. She's a teacher. You'll never get close.'

'No problem,' hooted Daz. 'With what Chesty's got you don't need to get close!'

*

Thursday 10th September
    Surprise, surprise. I'm not the only girl being

observant. As we walked to school today, Hayley told me with a giggle that she'd started as well. She'd observed that her legs were her best feature with her bum a close second. How about me?

Yes, I joked, I dedicated a whole page to what I think of the boys in our class. Her eyes lit up. What? What did you put? I left it blank, Hay!

She sighed and shook her head as if I was a bit mental, so to pay her back I didn't tell her what I really had written.

'Daz tells me you reckon Micro Mel's on the move at last,' said Greg Morris in the boys' changing rooms after Games. 'Sounds like I'll have to give her a look over.'

Wind-up time! thought Robbie at once. Getting Daz onto the subject of Chesty's assets was a laugh, but winding up Greg Morris was even better.

'Don't hang about then, Gregso,' he said. 'Because I'm definitely adding her to one of my lists. Probably only the C-list first off...'

'C-list?' Greg scowled, looking down his nose, hard-man style. 'What are you on about?'

'The girls, of course. The babes. Those on my A-list, like Zoë Freeman, I'm definitely going to get off with this term. Then there's my B-list – Ambrosia Skipper and the like. I'll start on them when I've finished working through the A-list.'

'And the C-list?'

'Possibles. Ones to keep an eye on.'

'You're talking out of the back of your head, Brookesie!' snapped Greg.

So easy! thought Robbie. *It's a wonder he wasn't born with a key in the middle of his back.* 'And you're talking out of your exhaust pipe, Gregso!'

'Break!' cried Daz, stepping in between them like a referee separating a pair of boxers.

From behind Friday's edition of the *Sporting Gazette* came the voice of Malcolm Atwill, son of Honest Terry Atwill, turf accountant and general money-bags.

'Well done, Daz. Let 'em slug it out later. That'll give me time to sell tickets.' The newspaper was lowered. 'In the red corner, Muscles Morris – six foot tall in his smelly socks. And in the blue corner, Bruiser Brookes, the Artful Dodger! Place your bets on the fight of the century!'

Daz made a disgusting noise. 'Fight? This pair? Powder-puffs at twenty paces, more like!'

Greg made to get Daz in an arm-lock, then thought better of it and slapped a hand against Twilly's newspaper instead. 'What are you studying that's so puffin' interesting, anyway?'

'Fillies, the same as you lot. Like Black Apple in the three o'clock at Goodwood this afternoon. Four to one she is. Good price that.'

Robbie told him where to stick his black apple, then followed up with, 'There's a difference between girls and horses, y'know!'

'Don't tell me,' said Twilly, folding his newspaper and placing it carefully in his leather briefcase. 'They've only got two legs.'

'And a few other differences, in case you haven't noticed!' yelled Greg. He swung back Robbie's way. 'So how far down your A-list have you got then, Brookesie? Come on, let's hear it.'

Robbie grinned. Bragging was one thing, but telling the truth was quite another! 'Sorry, Gregso. Another time, eh? I promised myself I'd follow Hayley McLeod to our tutor group meeting.'

'We followed her to French yesterday,' said Greg, still steaming. 'Her skirt isn't any higher today, is it?'

'Yeah, but our tutorial room is up two flights of steep stairs…'

Robbie was already on the move as he said it. Just as well. If he hadn't been, the others would have beaten him to the door. *Talk about quick off the mark*, he thought as they raced along. *Twilly should forget about Black Apple and put a fiver on us!*

*

Friday 11th September

Our first tutor group meeting of the term. Nothing much happened, so I spent my time making a few observations.

Observation: Our new year tutor is Ms Weston. She has the biggest bust in town, probably in the country and possibly in the known universe. If mine threatens to reach even half her size, I will head for a convent or a cosmetic surgeon as fast as my legs can carry me - which won't be very fast!

Observation: There are sixteen girls in our tutor group - and four boys. By the time Hayley and I arrived, they'd taken all the seats in the front row. Ms Weston was delighted! What a refreshing change to see them there, instead of skulking at the back. You can see things better at the front, Miss, said Darren Hogg. And she doesn't know what he's on about!

Afterwards, Hayley seemed a bit disappointed. Only four boys. Pity. Boys liven things up. I wish there were more of them. There are more of them, but they're all in the other tutor groups, thank God!

She shook her head in that funny way again. Be serious, Mel. You can't ignore boys, they're a fact of life. Of course I can't ignore 'em, Hay. They make too much noise for that!

'Sixteen babes in our tutor group!' hooted Daz as they spread themselves out under a tree near the netball courts. 'And just the four of us! What d'you think of that, lads?'

Twilly lowered his *Sporting Gazette*. 'I think that, statistically speaking, it's a very odd distribution.'

'A bit like Chesty, eh Daz?' hooted Robbie.

Greg was in dream-land. 'Sixteen divided by four equals four...'

'No need to show off just because you're in the top Maths group,' said Daz, aiming an apple core his way.

It missed, and Greg dreamed on. 'So, which four shall it be? Trick-ee.'

He was woken up with a cold dose of bookie-talk from Twilly. 'Ah, but it doesn't work like that, does it? If four horses go in for sixteen races they don't all win four each. Some win more and some win less...'

Robbie jumped in there. It was a wind-up-Greg opportunity that was too good to miss.

'And why's that?' he said. 'Because some are good-looking thoroughbreds like me and some are clapped-out also-rans like you, Gregso!'

Greg sneered and flicked back his hair like it was a

whip. 'You have got to be kidding, Brookesie. Kid-ding! If anybody's going to get those babes hopping it's going to be me. Because I've got what you haven't.'

'What's that? Fleas?'

'Girl appeal, of course. So it doesn't matter what Twilly's calculator says. I'll be getting more than my fair share.'

Twilly still hadn't started reading his *Sporting Gazette*. 'Aiming to get one of our tutor group fillies under starter's orders are you then, Greg?'

'Could be, could be.' He looked Robbie's way. 'Micro Mel, perhaps.'

'In your dreams!' honked Daz

The winder-upper had been given a taste of his own medicine. Before he knew it, Robbie was scoffing, 'You wanna bet?'

Bet. The instant the word was mentioned, Twilly dived in faster than a crocodile who'd just spotted a skinny-dipper paddling about in his river. Thinking about it later, Robbie realised he shouldn't have been surprised. With a dad like Honest Terry Atwill, a guy who'd take bets on two slugs crawling up a wall, some of it was bound to rub off.

'Lads,' said Twilly, 'I've just had me an idea. Remember in Year 7 we had that *Swimathon*?'

'Get sponsors and swim as many lengths as you can,'

nodded Daz helpfully.

'And last year we had that *Readathon*?'

Daz nodded again. 'Get sponsored to read as many books as you can. Went through all the Noddys, didn't I? Cost my old man a packet!'

'Well,' said Twilly, lips twitching at the corners, 'how about us holding our own little event this term...' He paused, making sure he'd got their undivided attention. He had. Especially when he said, '...a *Snogathon*.'

'A what?' blinked Greg.

'*Snogathon*,' said Twilly, coolly. 'Instead of Noddy books or lengths of the pool we go for snogs. With the winner scooping the kitty.'

Robbie sat up. 'Kitty? What kitty?'

'Money. Winnings. We each put in the same amount and the one who's been the most successful – by the end of term, say – takes the lot.'

'Namely me,' said Greg, looking Robbie's way.

Robbie just had to hit back. 'In that case you'll put up your loot straight off, won't you? How much you thinking of, Twilly?'

'A pony each.'

'What's that when it's not in bookie-speak?'

'Twenty-five pounds.'

'Twenty-five quid!' yelped Daz. 'That's...that makes...'

'A pot of one hundred smackeroonies,' smiled Twilly. 'So, lads, who's up for it? Daz?'

'A hundred-quid kitty? That's got to be worth thinking about...' He nodded, hard. '...I've thought about it. I'm in!'

'Greg?'

'I'm in if Brookesie's in.'

The crafty sprocket! thought Robbie. He hadn't expected that. What could he say? What else but to try and turn things round his way. 'And I'm in if you're in, Gregso.'

Twilly didn't give them a second chance. 'And I'm in as well. Good stuff, lads. This is going to brighten up the term no end!'

Robbie glanced at Greg. Was he going to argue? It didn't look like it. So how could *he*? The best he could do was mutter, 'What about the rules, then?'

Twilly raised an appreciative finger. 'Good point, Brookesie. I'll draft some out for early next week. In the meantime, lads, start raising your stake money!'

Second Week of Term
Starting Slowly

For his second-ever lesson with Robbie's class, Mr Carmichael led them outside. Not far, just past the kitchens and on through the overgrown conservation area to the chestnut tree near the netball courts.

'*Inspiration*,' said the teacher once they were all seated. 'Interesting word, that. It comes from the Latin *inspirare*, meaning *to breathe*. For the great poets, that's how important inspiration was – as important as breathing.'

It was an early chance, and Robbie grabbed it with both hands. 'That lets me out then,' he said, just loud enough, 'I've got asthma!'

Carmichael did no more than flick an eyebrow. 'Then we'll have to see if we can provide you with the poetic equivalent of an inhaler, won't we, Mr Brookes?'

He then spent the next half-hour pointing out things around them and quoting bits from poems off the top of his head.

'Thomas Peacock wrote, "I dug, beneath the cypress shade…"' Carmichael said. 'Emily Brontë wrote, "Fall, leaves, fall; die, flowers, away…"' The English teacher pointed across at the mess of a conservation area. 'And Edward Thomas was probably looking at a scene like this when he wrote, "Tall nettles cover up, as they have done..."'

Robbie yawned, looked at his watch, wondered if he could possibly stay awake much longer – and then, as Daz gave a low moan, realised he probably could. Over on the netball court, Ms Weston had bounced out to start her class.

'Form poems,' Carmichael was saying. 'A simple type of poem with lines of words in a numerical pattern. Example, anybody? How about you, Mr Hogg?'

'Forty-two, twenty-three, thirty-eight?' said Daz, goggling Ms Weston's way.

'Ambitious, Mr Hogg,' said Carmichael. 'You'll find a word pattern such as two, four and three a lot easier. That is, two lines, of four and three individual words. For example, a fine day like today might inspire the simple form poem:

Sky, heaven, space, blue.
Sun, gold, fire.'

Then he said, 'Who'd like to try and compose one? Miss Bradshaw?'

Robbie snapped his eyes away from the netball court

and across to where a flustered Melanie was struggling for words.

'Er...flowers, field, er...greenery, er...grass...'

As she dried up, in jumped a smirking Greg. 'Sit, down, pain-in-the-...'

'Thank you, Mr Morris!' interrupted Carmichael quickly. 'We get the idea.'

Beyond him, Robbie was pleased to see, Mel Bradshaw was giving Greg a look that would have curdled milk. Not all the girls were as disgusted, though. Mel's mate Hayley McLeod was giggling, her hand over her mouth.

Having stopped Greg in his tracks, Carmichael set about trying to make a final point. 'Poets don't simply dump words in thoughtlessly, Mr Morris. Try to be aware of the feeling of the piece.'

'After sitting out here,' muttered Robbie, 'I haven't got any feeling left in my piece.'

Monday 14th September

Poetry in the open air! Wild! Well it was until DC asked me to make up a form poem there and then. I had no inspiration at all. That's probably why I couldn't breathe!

Then, when I did get going, Greg Morris butted in with some stupid crack. It made Hayley laugh, but not DC. He gave me an apologetic look, as if to say don't worry Mel, old Wordsworth probably had to put up with dipsticks like this when he was daffodil-spotting.

Stupid, thick, gormless, dumb
who? them - boys!
How's that for a form poem!

*

Robbie loped along the corridor, not sure if he really wanted to be going where he was going. As good as his word, Malcolm Atwill had come up with some rules for the *Snogathon* and proposed that the four of them meet up straight after school to discuss them. He'd also insisted on top security, so they'd arranged to meet in the new multi-media, multi-purpose library. There was a small alcove in the corner that was hardly ever used. It was where they kept the books.

The minute they were gathered, Twilly snapped open his briefcase and pulled out a sheet of paper. Robbie whistled in amusement. It looked as if Twilly hadn't only devised some rules, he'd typed them into his PC and printed them out in the shape of a scroll, curly writing and all!

'Puffin' hell, Twilly,' said Daz. 'What is it, the American Consternation?'

'If you're going to do a thing, do it properly,' he said seriously.

'Where's our copies, then?' asked Robbie.

Twilly raised a finger of caution. 'Secrecy is paramount,' he said. 'When we're agreed I'll print out some more. Not before.'

If we're agreed, thought Robbie, fully expecting the whole idea to die a death within the next half-hour. He leaned forward to study the sheet as Twilly began to lead them through his rules.

'Rule One: all participants in the *Snogathon* will be sworn to absolute secrecy. Any breach of the aforesaid secrecy, in any form and howsoever caused, will result in the immediate disqualification of the guilty participant.'

Daz blinked. 'Yer what?'

'It means if you open your big mouth and tell anybody what's going on, you're out,' said Greg.

'If I can continue,' said Twilly. 'Rule Two, Sub-section One: the winner of the *Snogathon* will be the contestant scoring the most credits by the end of term.' He tapped the scroll quickly. 'And, before anybody asks, Rule Two, Sub-section Two: credits will be scored by making progress in a snogful encounter with a member of our tutor group.'

'Objection,' said Greg. 'There's no such word as "snogful", is there?'

'There is now,' said Twilly. 'I've just invented it.'

Daz grinned and said, 'Technically, Chesty's a member of our tutor group. What do I get if I sweep her into my arms?'

'Broken arms,' laughed Robbie.

'But no credits,' said Twilly, taking Daz seriously.

Greg sighed. 'Get on with it, eh? How do we score credits?'

'Rule Three: credits will be earned for snog duration to a maximum of sixty seconds.'

Greg flicked the ash off an imaginary cigarette. 'Going to cramp my style, that one. Why not sixty minutes?'

'Because even somebody with a mouth the size of yours can't snog and snorkel at the same puffin' time,' said Robbie.

'Suit yourself,' said Greg, shrugging his shoulders and winding Robbie up in one move, 'I'll settle for clocking up credits a minute at a time if that's all you can cope with, Brookesie.'

'Sorry, it doesn't work that way,' said Twilly. He turned back to the scroll. 'Rule Four: only the competitor's personal best score per individual female will count for the purposes of the *Snogathon*.'

'In puffin' English, eh?' moaned Daz.

'It means, once you've hit the minute mark with a babe the only way to score more credits is to move on to another one.'

Robbie couldn't resist the opportunity to out-Greg Greg. 'Love 'em and leave 'em, eh?' he sighed. 'Fair enough, Twilly. But that's going to mean me breaking a lot of hearts. A lot of hearts.'

Back came Greg, this time with a dirty smirk. 'How about if we get further than snogging, Twilly? Any bonus credits for hands that manage a Star Trek? Y'know, boldly going where no hand has gone before?'

Robbie hit yet another shot in the bragging battle. 'Or if I get dragged off to see the duvet cover my babe's made in Needlework? From the inside…'

'No credits for any activity other than snogging,' said Twilly firmly.

'In other words, no score even if we score,' honked Daz. 'Why's that then?'

'I thought it would make the final rule more acceptable,' said Twilly, focusing on the bottom of the scroll. 'Rule Five: credits will only be credited after the details of the snogful encounter have been verified by two witnesses.'

Slowly, the meaning of this last rule sank in. 'Witnesses?' croaked Greg, finally breaking the silence. He looked like he'd swallowed a fly.

'Purely for the purposes of corroboration,' said Twilly calmly. 'It's standard Jockey Club practice. Before the result of a race is confirmed the stewards look at a video recording to make sure there hasn't been any cheating, nobbling or other devious practice.'

'You mean there'll be two pairs of beady eyes trained on my every move?' squawked Greg.

He looked ready to explode. Seeing this, how could Robbie do other than chip in on Twilly's side?

'There's the timing to think about as well, Gregso,' he said, deadpan. 'I mean, somebody's got to time how long you keep going with whoever, haven't they? How you going to see your watch in the pitch dark in the back row of the Odeon?'

'Luminous hands?' said Greg, weakly.

He's on the way out, thought Robbie, hopefully. *Good job too. This is getting out of hand.* He waited for Greg to tell Twilly to stick his competition, confident that there was nothing Twilly could say that would change Greg's mind. Wrong. Twilly did it with a single word.

'Money,' he said. 'There's big money at stake here, Greg. Witnesses make sure nobody can make a false claim. Not that I'm suggesting anybody would try it on...'

And, to top it all, he looked at Robbie as he said it!

'Right,' said a determined Greg at once. 'Witnesses it is.'

Twilly smiled. 'So, lads. *Snogathon* rules. All in favour?'

It was crunch time. Even as he asked the question, Twilly was raising his hand. *Well, he's got to, hasn't he?* thought Robbie.

Daz quickly poked his own hand into the air.

Robbie looked at Greg. Greg looked at him. Neither of them moved – until, with a smirk, Greg raised one finger.

'Just waiting to see if there was going to be any competition,' said Robbie as he saw his own hand lift itself aloft.

Twilly clicked the rules back into his case. 'Excellent. Lads, we are now officially under starter's orders. One more meeting, I think, and the *Snogathon* can begin.'

'Another meeting?' cried Greg. 'What for?'

'To agree the handicaps, of course. Some of those babes are going to be a bigger challenge than others!'

*

Thursday 17th September

Emotion: worry. About me and Hayley. We've always been best buddies, but now I'm worried our interests could be drifting apart.

On the way in to school we'd hardly started discussing last night's tense episode of our favourite hospital soap The Surgeon, (droolworthy Dr Glen Redrow skilfully removes messily ruptured appendix but has he left his missing wedding ring in its place?) before she changed the subject to the boys in our tutor group.

Did I fancy any of them? Not just after breakfast, no, I laughed, thinking that would get her back on track again. No such luck. She ploughed on through the list.

Zoë Freeman reckons Greg Morris is quite sexy.

I bet she does. Zoë would think a tailor's dummy was sexy!

Ambrosia Skipper thinks Daz Hogg is quite good-looking in an ugly kind of way. I think she means he's rugged.

So's a brick wall. And conversing with him is just like talking to one!

Malcolm Atwill's got his own credit card.

Malcolm Atwill would sell his own mother for a fiver! Come to think of it, has anybody ever seen her?

Melanie, will you be serious!

I am being serious, Hay. They're all gomms. If I want to see a bunch of chimps playing the fool, I'll go to the circus.

What about Robbie Brookes, then? He's a circus chimp as well, is he?

No, he's not. Robbie Brookes is a total clown.

End note. Have just realised, after an hour's doodling, that an anagram of Dave Carmichael is IDEAL CAVE CHARM!

Emotion: surprise. I'm normally hopeless at anagrams!

*

Robbie spread himself uncomfortably across a bench seat in the book zone. Uncomfortably, because he'd been condemned to a whole day wearing his short, too-tight-crotched reserve pair of trousers after his mum had thrown his best pair in the wash the night before. All because of a slick of mud down one side caused by a sensational sliding tackle in the afternoon big match. Women!

He eased the situation round his lower parts by propping his feet up on a table. Greg and Daz were lounging on the seats opposite. In between them, Malcolm Atwill was hugging his briefcase like it was the crown jewels.

'Come on,' said Greg impatiently, 'what you got in there, the plans for World War Three?'

'Not quite,' said Twilly. He looked around, noted the usual Friday-afternoon emptiness of the place, and only then clicked open the catches on his case. 'But though I say it myself, this lot is pretty explosive stuff. Guard them with your lives.'

Out came a polythene folder. Robbie sat up, but

Twilly didn't immediately hand out what it was they were supposed to be guarding. Explanations first.

'Now, as I said before, not all the babes are going to be equally...*attainable*, shall we say.'

'Snoggable, you mean?' grinned Daz.

'Correct. Hence the need for Twilly's Individual Tariff System.' The polythene folder was flapped, but still not unloaded. 'A system to even things up. A bit like the handicapping system in horse-racing, where the better horses are given more weight to lug around the track.'

'That can't be right,' growled Greg. 'Amazon Adams is carrying more weight than all the other babes put together – but that makes her the worst bet, not the best.'

Twilly sighed. 'You know what I mean. In my scoring system the tough babes, the ones who are going to be hardest to get anywhere with, have higher tariffs. Pull one of them, and you score more credits.'

He was finally easing sheets out from the polythene folder. 'So, lads,' he said, handing them round, 'here are my proposals...'

In spite of trying to play it cool, Robbie's eyes went down faster than the *Titanic*. And what he saw was, he had to admit, impressive. Twilly had given them not only the *Snogathon* rules for reference but also, at the bottom, a full list of the girls in their tutor group.

Against each name was a number.

Zoë Freeman	10 credits per snog second (/ss)
Ambrosia Skipper	15 credits/ss
Emma Hamawi	16 credits/ss
Purity Meek	18 credits/ss
Laura Essex	19 credits/ss
Hayley McLeod	21 credits/ss

Then came the middle-order batting, those with tariffs between 25 and 45, until just one up from the bottom, Robbie saw:

Melanie Bradshaw   60 credits/ss

'So, let me get this right,' said Robbie. 'A ten-second turn with Micro Mel would score...'

'Ten seconds at sixty credits per second, six hundred credits,' responded Twilly before he'd even finished.

'The same as a full-length sixty-second session with ten-credits-per-second Zoë Freeman?'

'Correct.'

Greg nodded approvingly. 'Sounds about right. Rumour has it that Zoë's surname should really be get-it-for-Freeman.'

'Whereas Micro won't be easy,' said Daz. 'Not judging

by the looks she gave us when we plonked ourselves under Chesty's nose – well, not her nose exactly...'

Robbie glanced down at the list again. Just one name followed that of Melanie Bradshaw. The big one:

Sandra Adams   100 credits/ss

Nobody argued. A number twice that size wouldn't have made it worth tangling with the biceps of Amazon Adams.

Twilly was looking businesslike, clearly a breath away from telling them it was make-your-mind-up time. If the whole *Snogathon* idea was going to be shot down, thought Robbie, this had to be the moment.

His heart gave a little surge as Daz cleared his throat and said, 'Taking this a bit seriously, aren't you Twilly?'

'A hundred quid is serious money,' said Twilly.

It was all he'd needed to say. Within seconds, Daz and Greg had given their blessing to the tariffs.

With their eyes on him, Robbie knew what he had to do. Smile knowingly. Fold up his rules sheet nonchalantly. Slide it into his back trouser pocket casually. And say confidently, 'Looks like I'd better get me calculator warmed up, eh?'

'Then, lads,' said Twilly brightly, 'as we say in racing circles: they're off! I hereby declare the *Snogathon* officially started. May the best snogger win.) And, to make sure we all know what the score is, I volunteer to faithfully record the results of our efforts in here...'

Their guffaws, as they saw what Twilly had pulled out from his briefcase, earned a fierce glare from the librarian.

'Carmichael's log-book...? ' hissed Robbie. 'You're not!'

'And why not? If the *Snogathon* isn't going to be a spontaneous overflow of powerful feelings then I don't know what is!'

Twilly flipped the book open. Beneath Wordsworth's definition Robbie saw that he'd already drawn a table of five columns, each with its own heading:

Contestant	Date of Activity	Details of Claim	Credits Scored	Witnesses

'Lads,' said Twilly, 'I give you – the *Snog Log*!'

*

Twenty-five quid for a *Snogathon* entry fee was two weeks' pay for Robbie from his paper round at the Zygs'. He'd always called them that. The plate above their shop door actually read: *Zygmunt and Frieda Paszlowski, licensed to sell tobacco and intoxicating spirits*, but as he wasn't Polish and didn't have a double-jointed tongue he'd always called them Mr and Mrs Zyg.

Robbie liked them, even though they did pay him slave labour rates for hauling socking great bags full of newspapers round the streets on Saturday and Sunday mornings. They were a good laugh – Mr Zyg, especially.

Mr Zyg was a big bloke, barrel-chested. He had a bit of a limp, Robbie had noticed, which caused him to hang on to the counter now and again. But there was nothing limp about his lungs. Mr Zyg had a voice loud enough to make soup cans fall off the shelves; and fire-lighters and packets of assorted nuts and bolts – just about anything, because Zygs' wasn't simply a paper shop. Name it and they seemed to sell it. There was even a little mini-café section at the back of the shop where they served up teas and buns.

'Robbie!' boomed Mr Zyg as soon as he arrived. 'I have the complaint about you! Eighty-nine Bulawayo Avenue. He says he finds your fingerprints all over his magazine!'

Robbie didn't need reminding. Eighty-nine Bulawayo. *Daily Star, Sunday Times* and, once a month, plucked from the intriguing collection on a high shelf, an ultra-glossy magazine called *Starkers!*.

He was about to deny touching it, claim that the

milkman must have taken it out of the letterbox, ask for a hundred similar offences to be taken into consideration – all at once – when suddenly Mr Zyg roared with laughter.

'Joke! He not say that!' His face went deadpan. 'He said, next time you wear gloves!' Then his face cracked and, as he roared with laughter again, Robbie was sure he heard the windows rattle.

It was enough to bring Mrs Zyg bustling out from the café section at the back. She gave Robbie a big, natural smile. He smiled back, thinking not for the first time that, in a middle-aged kind of way, Mrs Zyg was a cracker. Thirty-five years ago she must have been really something. How she ended up with Mr Zyg was beyond him!

She wagged a finger under Mr. Zyg's nose. 'You playing silly boys again?'

Slowly and obviously, Mr Zyg took the latest *Starkers!* from the shelf and laid it on top of Bulawayo's paper. Mrs Zyg snatched it away. 'Gah. Mucky pup,' she said. 'Why you look at girls on front covers? You got me.'

'That *why* I look!' boomed Mr Zyg, winking at Robbie.

Mrs Zyg glared at him, then giggled. 'Impossible man!'

'Impossible woman!' laughed Mr Zyg.

He slid his arm round Mrs Zyg's waist. She did the same, except that her arms only stretched half-way round Mr Zyg's middle. They were like a pair of...well, Robbie didn't know what they were like a pair of, but he wished they wouldn't do it while he was around.

Why can't they act their age? You'd never see OM and Mum slobbering over each other in public, that's for sure.

Robbie had never even seen them do it in private.

Third Week of Term
Looking at Me

Carmichael was different, all right, Robbie had to admit that. While there was no chance of the teacher turning him into an English swot, even less of persuading him to scribble down pansy-wansy emotions in his little log-book, at least the bloke did try to liven things up...

'William Wordsworth didn't just spend his time sitting on grass banks turning out pretty poems, you know. He really wanted to join the French Revolution. Given the chance, he'd have been over there butchering aristocrats with the best of them.

'John Keats gave up a career in medicine to become a poet. Brave decision. And the critics hated his stuff. He died at the age of twenty-five, not knowing that one day he'd be really famous.'

Dead famous! thought Robbie, and would have said so if Carmichael hadn't immediately come out with some facts that took his mind off it.

'Samuel Taylor Coleridge was usually roaring drunk. Percy Bysshe Shelley was always running away from people he owed money to. And as for Lord Byron – he had more love affairs than you lot have had bags of crisps!'

Phew! thought Robbie. *I get through a bag a day and half a dozen at weekends!*

'So,' Carmichael challenged them, 'who thinks poets are boring?'

Robbie glanced around the room. Not a hand was in the air. Melanie Bradshaw and the rest of the babes seemed to be lapping it up and as for the lads – they were probably doing the crisp sums too.

'Well,' Carmichael went on, 'you, too, have what it takes to be poets.'

I have? thought Mel.

Cobblers, thought Robbie.

Nobody was calling him to be a poet. Especially a debt-ridden one like Percy Bash Shelley, or whatever his name was. He may have been feeling flat broke after giving Twilly his *Snogathon* stake money that morning but it was going to be a temporary feeling. When he ran out the winner, he was going to be quids in!

'And, like the great names I've just mentioned,' Carmichael was continuing to insist, 'you're not boring either. You may think you are, but you're not.'

He jabbed out a finger, pointing his way round the room. 'You, you, you, you, you...are an interesting person! So this week I want you to observe one person in particular – yourselves!'

*

Tuesday 22nd September

I tried looking at myself this evening, Dave. (Can I call you that? Nobody else will know.) It was a depressing experience. I'm coming to realise that I'm different to the other girls. And getting more different. I don't mean physically. Except for Sandra Adams, none of us looks really odd. And even poor Sandra doesn't look quite so bad when she's sitting down and not ducking through doors.

No, the difference is that this term the others have all become image-mad. Why? To make themselves attractive to boys! Boys now seem to be their main topic of conversation. It's boys this, boys that - and especially boys 'the other'! (If you want to hear emotional talk in the raw, Dave, stick your head round the door of our loos!)

That's why I'm starting to feel out of things. I want to carry on talking about the things we've always talked about, like TV soaps and horror films and pop stars' private lives. I don't want to discuss the gathering hairs on Darren Hogg's legs or debate the likelihood of Greg Morris's mum pressing creases in his boxer shorts. Am I the odd one, or are they?

*

They'd found the perfect girl-spotting spot. In the cafeteria it was, the table right opposite the till. It gave the lads maximum viewing time.

First they had the slow, rear-view, tray-sliding walk along the food counter.

Then came a full-profile stop at the cash-desk – fifteen seconds at least, more if they'd been chatting in the queue and hadn't got their money ready.

Finally there was another chance for all-round inspection as they grabbed their cutlery and roamed around looking for a spare seat.

'Brilliant, eh?' gloated Daz, whose idea it had been. 'Like a fast-food catwalk, it is here!' He gawped over at the counter. 'There's a tasty dish. Hot, spicy chilli and Zoë Freeman!'

Greg Morris smirked. 'I'll go for fishcakes, peas and Hayley Macleod, I think. Hang about, though...maybe I should make that pizza with a choice of toppings and Ambrosia Skipper.'

Malcolm Atwill peered over the top of his *Sporting Gazette*. 'Healthy option just coming, Gregso. Cauliflower cheese and Micro Mel.'

Greg rubbed his hands together. 'Too much, Twilly. I'm going to be spoilt for choice!' He looked at Robbie. 'Don't worry, Brookesie. I'll leave you something.'

Daz jerked a thumb at the girl who'd just collected her tray and was muscling her way through the crowds to a table in the far corner. 'Something like that?'

'Just like that, Dazzer!' said Greg. 'A lump of rhubarb crumble and an even bigger lump of Amazon Adams!'

Robbie felt a twinge of pity. *Poor old Amazon. There's always something on a menu that nobody fancies!*

Wednesday 23rd September

I am going to start bringing sandwiches. Today in the cafeteria I felt like I was taking a bath in an outsized goldfish bowl in the middle of Wembley Stadium. It was all I could do to stop myself dropping my tray to check the state of my buttons.

I'm fed up with being ogled, inspected, scrutinised, gawped at, examined, studied - and any other words in the dictionary that mean the same thing.

But it seems like I'm on my own again. The other girls don't mind. It's flattering, said Hayley, makes me feel like a film star. Purity Meek agreed with her. Big surprise - not. Before the goggling began she used to nip off home at lunchtime!

*

Robbie lay back on his bed and thought. He wouldn't have been sad to see the *Snogathon* drowned at birth, but now it was under way he was just going to have to put up a good performance. Better than Greg Morris, anyway. And Daz – he'd never let him forget it otherwise. And, puffin' hell, coming second to Twilly would be like Arsenal being knocked out of the FA Cup by Useless United of the Totally Useless League.

In other words – he just had to win the thing! How to go about it, though? Then it came to him. What did football managers do when their team was faced with a big match? Built up dossiers on their opponent's strengths and weaknesses, of course.

Robbie leaned over the side of his bed and peered underneath. Carmichael's log-book was still there, good as new. Well, apart from the orange stain caused by the half-eaten segment of pizza that also seemed to have found its way under his bed at some time in the past.

He pulled out the book and flipped it open. Twilly could use his as a *Snog Log*, if he liked. His was going to be put to a far better use! Crossing out big Willie Wordsworth's wonderful words, Robbie began writing.

Strengths and Weaknesses of *Snogathon* opponents:

Greg Morris
Strength: Fancies himself as a smooth Hollywood gangster and is getting better at the look. (He should be, he practises it every time he goes past a shop window.) It could impress babes who fancy living dangerously.

Weakness: Greg may look smooth, but get near him after games and you realise he can smell really rough. If he remembers to use his deodorant we could be struggling.

Daz Hogg
Strength: Plenty. He's got muscles where I've got pimples. Could appeal to babes who are scared of the dark and need a strong arm round them.

Weakness: With luck most babes will be even more scared of being in the dark with Daz!

Twilly
Weakness: Looks a bit like a weasel and on first impression he comes across as cold and calculating. The same goes for the second

impression, third impression, etc., etc.

Strength: His own credit card! Could attract babes who prefer money to good looks and are prepared to take their chances on ending up being sold to some Arab sheikh with even more money than Twilly.

Robbie sat back. What now? Look at himself, of course. How did he compare to the opposition?

Not easy. How do you look at yourself? Was he smoother than Greg, for instance? Tougher than Daz? Did he own a bigger wallet than Twilly? No, to all three.

Then he remembered part of his report at the end of Year 8:

Robert's behaviour, his Year Head had written, *is good when supervised, but I'm afraid he can act rather foolishly at other times.*

The OM had loved it. 'Chip off the old block,' he'd crowed.

Me, myself, Robbie Brookes
Weakness: None.

Strength: Doesn't take anything too seriously. Not a swot. Game for a laugh and a giggle. Got to be a winning combination!

He slapped the book shut. Puffin' hell, without thinking about it he'd done what Carmichael had asked them to do and looked at himself!

*

Friday 25th September

Emotion: satisfaction at my growing powers of observation.

Just as we were leaving, I observed Dave Carmichael carrying a pile of poetic-looking papers across the playground and into the car park. Like the colour of his shirt, said Hayley, aubergine is this year's hot hue.

Another growing difference. Hayley is becoming very fashion-oriented. I'm not. OK, so I noticed the shirt was short-sleeved with three-button fastening, his check jeans had frogmouth pockets, his socks were more deep purple than aubergine and his black leather moccasin casuals were slightly worn down on the outside of the right heel, but that's only because I was being observant.

Anyway, I was more intent on watching DC putting the poetic-looking papers into the rear of his car. It was a very nicely shaped rear. The car's wasn't bad either!

Emotion: ooo-er!

*

Robbie's papers weren't ready for him when he turned up at the Zygs' on Saturday morning.

No wonder, he thought. He could hear the pair of them giggling away in the storeroom they used for marking up. To pass the time he sneaked a quick look at the *Starkers!* body-of-the-month for September, a blonde draped over the bonnet of a car. Next thing he knew the giggling had stopped and Mrs Zyg was looking over his shoulder.

'Fine bodywork, yah?' she cackles.

Robbie felt his face catch fire. 'The car!' he burbled. 'I was looking at the car!'

'Course you were, Robbie!' She roared with laughter, embracing Mr Zyg as he limped up. 'Is what my man says. I study the bodywork, love!'

'That why I test your rear seat so often,' boomed Mr Zyg, pinching her bum, 'to check it not getting too padded!'

'Hah! Hark who talks!' Mrs Zyg turned to Robbie. 'Can you believe this man was slim when we meet? And so light on the feet! The dancer of my youth, Robbie. The dancer of my youth.'

Robbie grinned at huge, limpy Mr Zyg. 'Not any more, eh?'

Mr Zyg folded his arms across his barrel of a stomach, glowering and twinkling at the same time. 'What you mean, not any more?' he roars. 'I still twinkle-toes. Better than old skinny-legs here!'

Sweeping his wife off her feet and into his brawny arms, Mr Zyg whirled her round in the air, making her hair fly out. For a moment it was as if his gammy leg didn't exist. Gliding forwards, looking deep into her eyes, the burly man steered his wife backwards like they were on the ballroom floor.

Then he tried a fancy spin and to the watching Robbie it was as if Mr Zyg's bad leg suddenly hadn't wanted to know. Toppling to one side, Mr Zyg just managed to turn himself so that it was his back that crashed into the shop counter and not Mrs Zyg's. As he leaned against it to recover, she broke free and raced into the café part for a chair.

He dropped down on it so hard Robbie half expected to see the thing give way. Mrs Zyg crouched down beside him as he puffed and panted. Robbie assumed he was only out of breath, but she looked really anxious.

'You OK?' whispered Mrs Zyg. 'Tell me.'

Mr Zyg forced a grin. 'Fine, fine.' He reached out and put the palm of his hand against her cheek. 'Hey. I still your dancer, yah?'

She smiled and nodded. 'Yah. You still my dancer.'

And Robbie smiled too.

*

His Sunday round usually took an hour longer than Saturday – even a *Starkers!* Saturday. All the papers had supplements. Some of them even had supplements to the supplements. It was ridiculous. His bag couldn't have weighed much more if they'd stuck the trees in it instead.

Afterwards he went back to the shop to collect his pay – only to find Mr and Mrs Zyg cuddling and giggling again. Then it was back home to a different atmosphere altogether.

Robbie couldn't understand it. The OM was a complete opposite to Mr Zyg. He was pretty good-looking, kept his suntan topped up, had his hair highlighted, trimmed and scrunched as regular as clockwork and wouldn't dream of going out of the door wearing gear without a designer label on it. OK, so he could spend a bit less time drinking with his mates, but he didn't see why it bothered his mum as much as it did.

The argument they had that day was typical. The OM had bowled in whistling, jacket slung over his shoulder.

'You were supposed to be back a couple of hours ago,' glared Robbie's mum.

'So?'

'So now your dinner's ruined.'

'Not hungry anyway. Had something while I was out, didn't I?'

'Where?'

'The Rose and Crown.'

'No you didn't. It's closed for refurbishment, I drove past it the other day.'

'So I went there first then on to the Red Lion!' yelled the OM. 'What is this, an interro-bloody-gation?'

And they were off. Robbie hurried upstairs to bury himself in his *Graveyard III* computer game – *can you survive the terrors of the night?* – for as long as it took. By the time he'd fought his way through to Decomposition Level the shouting was over. But if past form was anything to go by, he knew, the silence only meant they wouldn't be talking to each other all evening.

His Carmichael log-book was now tucked away safely in a drawer. He pulled it out. What was that quote they'd been given on the first day? He looked at the now crossed-out lines:

> 'Poetry is the spontaneous overflow
> of powerful feelings...'

In that case their house should be crawling with poetry. The OM and his mum had got enough powerful feelings for a dozen poets!

And Robbie found himself thinking: *So have I when they start. I want to scream at the top of my voice: 'Stop it! Stop it!'*

Sunday 27th September

Make notes on what makes you happy, Dave said. Today made me happy. Mall-mooching with Hayley, meeting up with Zoë and the others, getting back home in time for Dr Redrow and the omnibus edition of The Surgeon - magic.

And afterwards Hayley only wandered off the subject once. If you liked somebody but you weren't sure if they liked you, she said, would you say something and hope they did like you or say nothing in case they didn't and never would after that because you'd asked them?

Come again?

Never mind. Do you think Dr Redrow should be tucking his stethoscope in his top pocket or letting it dangle?

Fourth Week of Term
Opening the Score

Monday 28th September

Emotion: happiness, continued!

#1 Happy for Hayley. She's solved her problem, not that I know what it was! Do you believe in girl-power, Mel? she said on our walk in. Y'know, girls deciding what they want and going for it?

You bet, Hay. So what do you want?

She giggled. Tell you later. Except - it's not what. It's who...

#2 Happy for me! One thing had been bugging me since last week. The poets Dave had told us about - Wordsworth, Keats, Coleridge, Shelley, Byron - what were they? Men, the lot of them! Where were the great female poets? So what did Dave do today? Quote one, that's all! Talk about being on the same wavelength!

'Christina Georgina Rossetti,' said Carmichael. 'Born in London, she lived to be sixty-four, but wrote her first verses when she was twelve years old.'

Robbie stuck his hand up. 'Bet she didn't get to

Ectoplasm Level of *Graveyard III* though!'

Carmichael nodded slowly. 'True, Mr Brookes. She wouldn't have had a *ghost* of a chance of beating you in that respect!'

We'll call that one a draw, thought Robbie. They'd both got a laugh – but he'd got the respect of the lads: most of them were still stuck on Interment Level!

'This is one of Christina Rossetti's poems,' Carmichael went on. 'It's called "A Birthday". It shows her great observational powers – and something else you should all be able to spot for yourselves.' He started reading.

'My heart is like a singing bird
   Whose nest is in a watered shoot;
My heart is like an apple tree
   Whose boughs are bent with thick-set fruit;
My heart is like a rainbow shell
   That paddles in a halcyon sea;
My heart is gladder than all these
   Because my love is come to me.'

'Well?' said Carmichael as he finished. 'Did you notice anything about the style of writing?'

'It's got a lot of heart, Mr Carmichael!'

'Thank you, Mr Brookes. Very original. Anything else?'

'A steady beat?'

'It uses the device known as the *simile*, Mr Brookes. The poet compares her heart to three powerful images of great happiness, fuller, for instance, than a branch laden with apples.'

'Apples? Really? Cor!'

Emotion: despair

For you, Dave. I don't know about Christina Rossetti's heart, but mine bleeds for you. Teaching prawns like Robbie Brookes must be like pushing peas uphill with your nose.

Hey, that's a simile!

Bumping into Mr Carmichael was a complete accident. If he'd known the teacher was going to be standing at the vending machine, Robbie would have taken a different route to the library. Meeting the guy once a week was starting to become bearable, but twice in a day was too much.

But on the way to the library he'd been – 'Lads, we should have a weekly progress meeting. This is a serious business,' Twilly had said – and beside the vending machine Carmichael had been.

Robbie put his head down and speeded up, but Carmichael stepped into his path.

'Mr Brookes...'

Not knowing the penalty for flattening teachers, but assuming it was pretty bad, Robbie stopped. Besides, Carmichael didn't look like he was going to give him an earful. And he didn't. He stunned him instead.

'As you demonstrated again in today's lesson, Mr Brookes, you have a way with words. Have you ever thought of applying that talent to poetry?'

'Er...not really.'

'Think about it. You might surprise yourself.'

Carmichael wasn't looking for a discussion. Having said his bit, he turned back to studying the menu on the vending machine.

Robbie headed on up the stairs towards the library, scoffing to himself so hard that he completely ignored the person coming down.

Become a serious boff, Carmichael? You must be joking! Boffs don't pull the babes. It's chat that grabs them, not brains!

Mel reached the bottom of the stairs just as Carmichael succeeded in persuading the vending machine to cough up the mixed salad sandwich he was after.

She stopped.

He nodded and smiled. *Mixed salad sandwich*, she noticed at once. *Vegetarian? Could explain his clear complexion, healthy-looking hair, not to mention that firm bum...*

She just had to say something. 'Cool lesson today, Mr Carmichael.'

'Thank you, Miss Bradshaw. No problems, then? Everything clear?'

Mel tried to look like a girl whose eyes have been opened, etc., etc., a girl of maturity beyond her years, etc., etc.

'Fine...' she began, only to hear herself add, 'except that I'm kind of stuck on a couple of things. Can I come and see you about them?'

Why had she said that? Why had the thought of a spot of one-to-one tuition with Dave Carmichael suddenly burst into her mind like a glorious firework?

'Of course. Er...how about Friday at one o'clock?'

One in the afternoon, two in the morning – any time, Dave!

Up in the library, the *Snogathon* meeting hadn't started. Seconds after Robbie flopped into his usual seat, the sound of clashing hockey sticks had caused Daz to spin round and look out of the window.

'Look at that,' he breathed.

Down below, Ms Weston was putting the hockey team through their paces in a tight shirt that looked like it had a couple of struggling balloons trapped inside.

'Can we get started?' asked Twilly.

Reluctantly, Daz turned away. 'That's another bouncy memory for my records, anyway.'

'Your what?' said Greg.

'My records. My memories of Chesty in all her glory. Otherwise known as my Carmichael log-book.'

Robbie nearly choked. 'You're not using it to write about her!'

'Wanna bet? By the time I've finished, that book's going to be just like Chesty herself. Bulging!'

The meeting forgotten, Greg made a grab for Daz's bag to see if his book was in there. Daz responded by trying to give him a right hook. Robbie, diving for cover, tripped over Twilly's briefcase and collided with a display stand – and that was it.

Storming over to find out what was going on, Mrs Boothroyd, demon librarian, slung them out.

'Where are we going now?' asked Twilly.

'Home,' said Robbie.

'Yeah, it's too early for a meeting. The *Snogathon*'s only just started. We don't need one yet.'

'Yes we do.' Greg looked smug. He waited, milking the moment. 'Guess who's about to get off the mark, then?'

*

Robbie led the way to the Zygs' shop. It was on the way home anyway, and if he was going to have to suffer Greg Morris gloating, he might as well suffer it in a cheerful atmosphere. Besides which, bringing in a few extra customers wouldn't do him any harm next time he got into wage negotiations with Mr and Mrs Zyg.

'My, my,' boomed Mr Zyg as they jangled through the door, 'we have the full house!'

Robbie was kind of relieved to discover that for once he hadn't got Mrs Zyg locked in a clinch. Maybe they saved them up for the weekends. He led the others into the café area, where Mrs Zyg was wiping down the tables.

'Robbie!' she cooed. 'These are your friends? Lovely to see you all! Have some squashes on me!'

'Sounds good!' boomed Mr Zyg, and looped one of his huge arms round her waist. She slapped him away with a happy laugh.

'Squashes. Not squeezes, impossible man!'

Mr Zyg chuckled as he limped back into the shop. 'Would you believe? Thirty-over years and I still have trouble with the English.'

'And I still have trouble with the Polish!' Mrs Zyg called after him.

They spread themselves round one of the tables in

the café area. After Mrs Zyg had served up four tall glasses, Greg broke the bad news.

'Hayley McLeod. Asked her at break, didn't I?' He wet a finger and marked a score in the air. 'Looks like my first credit's in the bag, lads.'

'Not without witnesses,' said Robbie, hoping the reminder might wipe the grin off his face. No chance. A bomb under his chair wouldn't have done it.

'We're going to the flicks,' said Greg. 'Rialto, seven o'clock Thursday. *Claws of the Ripper.* That should get her screaming to be saved.'

'Who are your observers going to be?' asked Twilly, businesslike as ever.

'I'm easy,' shrugged Greg. 'Any volunteers?'

Robbie was ready to tell him what he would really enjoy volunteering to do for Greg when suddenly the thought struck him that here was a chance to continue his football management approach. He could watch the opposition! Trying not to sound too eager, he said, 'Put me down for one if you like.'

Daz raised a finger. 'And me. I haven't seen *Claws of the Ripper.*'

'You're not going to, either,' snapped Greg. 'I'm not having you pair skulking around in the dark while I'm getting warmed up. You can be waiting outside for us when it ends.'

'Where?'

'The phone box opposite the bus stop. We'll be catching the bus home.'

'We'll be there, Gregso,' winked Daz. 'Watching...'

'And timing...' said Robbie, throwing in the best wind-up comment he could manage under the circumstances: '...unless she requests you to stop instead of the bus!'

But Greg won even that skirmish. 'Stop? Never, Brookesie. It'll be more like, "Hold tight, please!".'

*

Tuesday 29th September

Emotion: sadness.

It's the beginning of the end. My best friend has got a boyfriend. She decoded her private riddle the moment we met, saying she was the person who hadn't been sure if somebody liked them, but after I'd agreed with her about girl-power she'd decided to go for it and when she'd seen the person on their own yesterday at afternoon break she'd gone for it and asked the person and the person did like her and she was going out with him on Thursday, him being Greg Morris.

Wednesday 30th September

Emotion: rapidly changing from sadness to

boredom - because Hayley's so sad!

She was on about this date with Greg Morris all day.

What shall I wear, Mel?

A blindfold?

I know, the green two-piece suit I got for my birthday!

Perfect, Hay. He's bound to love you in your birthday suit.

Thursday 1st October

I'm worried, Mel. What if he tries to kiss me?

You'll be even more worried if he doesn't try to kiss you, Hay!

That's true. I guess I'm just nervous.

So am I, Hay - with more reason. You've only got to fend off Grappling Greg Morris tonight. I've got to think up some sensible simile questions to ask Dave Carmichael tomorrow afternoon!

Emotion: nervous anticipation.

Robbie was having trouble opening the front door. His ribs hurt and he couldn't lift his arms properly. The door key wouldn't stay still long enough for him to shove it in the lock – not that he could see the lock too clearly, on account of his streaming eyes.

He wiped his eyes, controlled his limbs, ignored the pain and finally managed to get the door open and stagger up the stairs. Collapsing onto his bed, he closed his eyes. Hopeless. That only brought the scene flooding back and had him howling with laughter again.

There was only one thing he could think of doing. He pulled out his Carmichael log-book. Through the tears, Robbie cast his mind back over the timetable of that evening's events...

7.00: Me and Daz get to the Rialto for the start of *Claws of the Ripper*. We hide in the shadows so Greg doesn't spot us. We don't care what he said, we're planning to watch them watching the film.

7.05: Greg turns up. He's had cosmetic surgery on his hair. It's all spiky. He shoves an extra-strong mint in his gate and starts pacing up and down.

7.20: The film's about to start and the sucker's still pacing!

7.21: Hayley finally shows. She's been waiting in the foyer all the time 'cos she hadn't recognised him with his new hairdo!

7.26: As they slide into their seats, we slide into ours – three rows behind. *Claws of the*

Ripper begins, but we're more interested in watching Greg try and get his claws into Hayley.

7.41: He makes his first attempt! He leans towards her, anyway. Hayley fends him off with the tub of popcorn she must have bought while she was hanging around in the foyer!

8.33: The popcorn takes them the best part of an hour to finish! 'Must have been the last-you-through-*Titanic* size,' gurgles Daz.

8.45: I'm just thinking that if Greg wants a practice run before the bus stop he'll have to make a move soon when he leans a casual elbow on the back of Hayley's seat! She looks his way – and he scratches his ear!

8.56: He tries again, stretching a whole arm along the back of Hayley's seat this time. His hand creeps towards her shoulder like a pink tarantula. But just as he makes his move Hayley leans forward to scratch her knee, then leans back again. Greg's hand gets flattened!

9.04: Greg's still examining his fingers for broken bones. Me and Daz are nursing cracked ribs!

9.06: The crafty sprocket plays for

sympathy! He's whinged so much, Hayley's started caressing his hand. Before you can say Florence Nightingale he declares it fit again – and slides it smoothly round her shoulders!

9.14: She leans her head against him. Any second now...

9.15: Lights go up. End of film! Coughing and spluttering, me and Daz barge our way out before we die laughing or get spotted or both.

9.23: Arrive at phone box near the bus stop. We climb inside and wipe our eyes so we can see the next bit properly.

9.25: Greg and Hayley head our way. His arm's still twined round her shoulders like poison ivy. They stop at the stop. She looks up at him. He looks down at her. Slowly his lips descend like a space pod approaching the surface of the moon, until...

'Houston,' drawls Daz, 'the Eagle has landed. Start the clock.'

9.29: In quick succession, Greg scores with a two-second peck, a five-second dawdle and, his best effort so far, an impressive sixteen-seconder which looks like going the distance until Hayley needed to cough.

9.31: Another personal best! A twenty-three-second belter, with a thumbs-up in our direction half-way through!

'He's looking good,' says Daz grudgingly. 'Reckon he'll go for maximum with the next one.'

9.32: Greg goes for it.

9.32 and 10 seconds: Hayley's bus draws up!

9.32 and 20 seconds: Greg still going for it. Hayley's not made a move towards her bus. Either she's gone stone deaf or Greg is covering her ears with the stranglehold he's got her in.

9.32 and 28 seconds: Hayley breaks away.

9.32 and 29 seconds: Hayley runs after bus!

9.33 Hayley in tears. Greg calls taxi and forks out what looks like a lot of loot...

What an entry! thought Robbie. Carmichael would have been proud of him! No way was it going to inspire any poetry, but writing it all down had helped get it out of his system. At least he'd stopped gurgling uncontrollably.

What's more, he realised, he now had a permanent record he could shove under Greg's ski-jump nose whenever he needed the ultimate wind-up. Because, without any doubt, that *Snogathon* encounter was something Greg was not going to want reminding about!

*

It was £6.20 they'd seen Greg coughing up for the taxi, Robbie discovered next day. Plus £5.60 to get them both into the Rialto!

'Eleven pounds eighty altogether,' grinned Robbie, rubbing it in. 'For how many credits?'

Twilly's calculator seemed to appear from thin air. 'Twenty-eight seconds times a tariff of twenty-one...five hundred and eighty-eight.'

Robbie leaned over and punched a few buttons himself. 'Divided into eleven pounds eighty, makes... near enough twenty pee a credit. Gregso, at this rate you're going to spend more than you'll win!'

A squeezed-lemon look crossed Greg's face. 'More than I'll win? Conceding defeat already are you, Brookesie?'

It was a good one, Robbie had to admit that. Because, expensive or not, the sprocket had at least got an entry in the *Snog Log* of nearly 600 credits. And that was 600 more than him!

'Miss Bradshaw. Come in. Nice to see you. Have a seat.'

Dave Carmichael had his own little corner of the English Department staff room. It amounted to a tiny desk cluttered with thick books and poetic-looking papers, but to Mel it all looked terribly impressive. Impressive, but not nerdish. A half-full *Wallace and Gromit* mug tucked away in one corner showed her that for all his learning, Dave was just a regular guy.

'So, Miss Bradshaw. What aren't you clear about?'

My feelings for you, Dave!

'Similes,' said Mel. 'I get the hang of them, but it all turns a bit wobbly when I try to lump in emotion as well. How do you do that?'

It sounded so pathetically like what it was – the only half-sensible question she'd been able to come up with – that she wouldn't have blamed him if he'd said buzz off and stop wasting my time, but he didn't. Instead, she felt, he made it seem like the most intelligent question he'd ever been asked in his life.

'Right,' he said. 'Do you remember what I said about inspiration and breathing? Well, air is all around you. So inspiration is all around you, too. Look...' He dipped a hand into a carrier bag at the side of his chair. 'What's this?'

'A tin of red kidney beans.'

If she was honest, Mel would have said it kind of took the edge off the moment – but only until Dave Carmichael said, 'My rage is like a kidney bean, flushed red with anger!'

He placed his hand on the top of the tin, making her wish her knee was the sell-by date. 'You try,' he said.

'My...er...' stammered Mel, 'my heart is like a kidney bean...b-bursting with love.'

'Excellent!'

Lobbing the beans back into his bag, Dave Carmichael leaned across his desk and pulled a hand written scrap from beneath a magnet on the side of a metal filing cabinet. It was a poem.

'How do I love thee? Let me count the ways.
I love thee to the depth and breadth and height
My soul can reach...'

'Elizabeth Barrett Browning wrote those words to her husband,' he said.

Another female poet! Yes!

'She's taking love and comparing it to the largest space she can imagine. It's her way of saying it's impossible to measure how much she loves him. Read on. There's a simile in the seventh line.'

'I love thee freely, as men strive for Right...'

'Men fight for a just cause because their hearts won't let them do anything else. Elizabeth compares her love to that. Her heart won't let her do anything other than show how much she loves him. Get the idea?'

'Y-yes,' gulped Mel. 'Yes, I do.'

'Good. Now if you'll excuse me, Miss Bradshaw, I must have a caffeine injection before I face 10C.'

He returned the sheet to its magnet. Leaving him to his kettle and *Wallace and Gromit* mug, Mel wandered out into the corridor in a daze. It was only as she skipped away down the corridor that some more questions popped into her mind.

That poem under your magnet wasn't a photocopy, Dave. It was in somebody's handwriting. Whose was it? Who's counting the ways they love you?

Friday 2nd October
A Simile:
My heart is like a racing cycle
Whenever I think of Dave Carmichael!
Emotion: censored!

*

If he'd been in the mood, Robbie might just have joked to Twilly that Greg was starting to remind him of the dog who tried to get away from his owner on account of how he'd extended his lead.

But he wasn't in the mood for it. Witnessing Greg hit maximum, one minute's worth of credits with Hayley

McLeod, had put paid to that. What's more, this time it hadn't cost Greg a penny!

It had been a smooth performance, Robbie couldn't deny that. Arranging for him and Twilly to be on hand, Greg had taken Hayley for a walk round the perfumed garden in the park. Three o'clock had been the scheduled time and he'd had her there on the dot, his arm locked round her waist like it was a wheel clamp.

Guiding Hayley through the gate and into the garden, Greg hadn't aimed for the nearest bench. Instead, he'd trundled her over to one in the far corner. Only after they'd dodged from bushy shrub to bushy shrub until he and Twilly were close enough to hear as well as see, did Robbie realise why.

'Remembered what old Carmichael said about similes and all that stuff, didn't I, Hay?' he heard Greg dribble, 'and then I just knew I had to bring you here.'

'Oh, Greg! Really!'

Robbie peered through the greenery. Greg had dragged her to within sniffing distance of a rose bed. And for all her protestations, Hayley was lapping it up!

'My love is like a red, red, rose...' he heard Greg ooze.

'Oh, you are romantic ' sighed Hayley.

And that was it. Before Robbie could say 'puke', he saw their lips connect like a couple of sink plungers. Twilly started timing. Sixty seconds later Greg had posted the first *Snogathon* maximum score. Twilly, accounting satisfied, slid away.

Robbie was about to follow when he realised that Greg must have finally prised his lips away from Hayley's. Either that or he had the potential to be a very good ventriloquist, because he was talking again.

'Time to go, Hay,' Robbie heard Greg say.

Hayley's sigh spoke volumes. 'Already? We've only just got here.'

'I know, but...well, I've got a lot of reading to do, Hay. Sunday papers are an essential if you want to find out what's been moving and shaking in Wall Street. It's not far off a full-time job preparing to be a City whizz, y'know...'

City whizz? Who's he trying to kid? Robbie peered through the bushes. There was Greg, looking like his heart was cracking – and there was Hayley, soaking it up like a sponge!

'I understand, Greg. Just so long as you can find some time for me...'

'I will, Hay. I'll always find time for you...'

The oily sprocket! He's hit maximum and he's already got his dump-Hayley line worked out!

Fifth Week of Term
Counting Legs...

Monday 5th October
  English 2-3 p.m.
  Dave Carmichael was away, unwell. He sent a message from his sick-bed asking us to study Elizabeth Barrett Browning's poem, 'How DO I Love Thee?'. I started to do it. The boys started playing the fool.
  Emotion: my rage was like a kidney bean, flushed red with anger!
  That's why I smacked Darren Hogg in the mouth.

Robbie hadn't planned to take Carmichael's advice to try a bit harder at English. Even if he had, it would have quickly been scrapped once Chesty Weston had made her fleeting appearance to report that the great man was on his death-bed and that his last recorded words were asking them to study a poem by Elizabeth Brown Boots or somebody.

Beside him, Daz watched Chesty disappear and groaned quietly, 'Come back, Chesty! This poem will be the death of me. I need the kiss of life...'

Grabbing a sheet of paper, Robbie drew a big heart with an arrow through it and wrote 'Darren luvs Chesty' in the middle.

Then, having second – and more inspired – thoughts, he changed the wording to 'Darren luvs Chesty's' instead.

That was when it all got a bit out of hand. Daz saw what he'd written. Snatching up the sheet, he screwed it into a ball. From behind, Greg snatched the ball away from him. Whirling round, Daz made a grab for him. A brief scuffle, and the ball fell into the aisle. Robbie did what came naturally and gave it a kick. The ball shot off across the room, coming to rest beneath Melanie Bradshaw's chair.

'Thanks a bunch, Brookesie,' grinned Daz.

Robbie assumed he was being sarcastic – until Daz winked, and he realised he'd meant it. He'd just given him a perfect excuse to chat up Micro Mel!

Off Daz strolled. But Mel seemed to be totally engrossed in what she was doing. When Daz arrived at her side she didn't even look up. Everybody else had noticed, though. It all went quiet as Daz dropped to his knees beside her and placed a hand on his heart.

'How do I love thee, Melanie? Let me count your legs...'

Pretty good for Daz! thought Robbie.

What happened next wasn't so good for him,

though. Reaching out, Daz started to run his hand around Melanie Bradshaw's ankles searching for the ball of paper. That was when it happened. Obviously getting the wrong idea completely, Micro dropped her pen and smacked him round the face!

In Robbie's experience, trying to budge Daz in a rugby scrum was like tackling a stubborn hippo. But Mel's sudden swing had caught him off balance. He keeled over, then leaped to his feet like a prize fighter who doesn't want to show he's been hurt. Trouble was, he looked like a prize fighter too. He'd gone red in the face and, worse, his right fist was clenched tight.

Now Robbie knew his fist was only clenched because that incriminating ball of paper was inside it. Greg, too. But not Amazon Adams. No, she definitely did not know that. From the way she flew into the thick of things, it was perfectly clear to Robbie that Amazon thought Daz was about to trade punches with Micro.

With a movement that would have seemed quick from a normally sized girl, let alone a small mountain, Amazon grappled Daz into a neck-lock.

'Disgusting little toad,' she growled, giving Daz a vicious twist that made him gasp like a deep-sea diver who'd just had his air supply cut off.

'Pick on somebody your own size, Daz!' yelled Greg.

Amazon put her knee in the small of Daz's back.

Then, with a violent thrust, she sent him hurtling down the centre aisle to land slap-bang in Zoë Freeman's lap.

Could be worse, thought Robbie. *At least he made a soft landing!*

But, it seemed, it wasn't Daz's day. Before he'd had half a chance to get settled, in marched Chesty, took one look at the pair of them and dished out a detention each for straight after school.

No doubt about it. Carmichael was going to have a tough act to follow when he got back. That just had to be the best lesson of the term!

English. Observed big-time that Mel Bradshaw's got hidden depths – and I'm not referring to the contents of her B-cups. I'm talking about her size-DD temper!

*

Things were getting worse by the minute. He should have guessed, thought Robbie, the moment the cans were popped in the Zygs' café and Twilly opened the weekly *Snogathon* review meeting.

'I propose...' began Twilly.

'Malcolm! Sweetie!' Daz broke in at once. 'This is so sudden! But, no, I can't marry you. I'm spoken for.'

Daz sounded so chirpy, Robbie wouldn't have believed it was only twenty-four hours since he'd been humiliated by the Micro Mel / Amazon Adams tag team if he hadn't seen it with his own eyes. Then what Daz had said sank in.

'What do you mean, spoken for?'

'Zoë Freeman,' leered Daz. 'Chatted her up during detention, didn't I? So keep some time free for a bit more observing, Brookesie!'

It was bad news. And, of course, if anyone was going to twist the knife it was going to be Greg.

'Don't worry, Brookesie. At least I won't be calling on you for a couple of days. Not till I've ditched Hayley.'

'Ditched her?'

Greg sighed theatrically. *'Mais oui.* I mean, now I've hit maximum credits the girl's got to go...'

Robbie didn't feel good. All he needed now was for Twilly to come out and say he was lined up as well. Thankfully, he didn't. The contest administrator was still wanting to finish what he'd started.

'I propose,' repeated Twilly, 'a tariff revision. Two tariff revisions, to be precise. Melanie Bradshaw and Sandra Adams. After yesterday's little performance, I'd say that any kind of success with either of them will be extremely difficult...'

'And extremely painful,' said Daz, rubbing the small bruise on his chin.

'So I propose that both have their tariffs increased,'

said Twilly. He gave uthem the details. 'Agreed?'

Three nods. 'Agreed.'

'And that's it,' he added, seriously. 'No more revisions allowed. They stay the way they are for the remainder of the *Snogathon.* Agreed?'

Daz and Greg shrugged. 'Agreed.'

'Yeah, yeah, agreed.' said Robbie. *Who cares? It doesn't matter, does it?*

But it did matter. As he was to discover much later, it mattered a great deal...

Robbie's door was shut tight. It hadn't helped. He could still hear the OM shouting as he logged what they'd agreed to:

Mel Bradshaw's tariff up from 60 to 90.
Sandra Adams' tariff up from 100 to 150.
All tariffs now frozen.

Downstairs the argument was getting worse. He had no idea what had started it off, but it was turning into one of the nasty ones. Snatches of it pierced the music from his stereo headset even with the volume turned up.

'Where were you this afternoon?'

'Office.'

'Vince, they said you'd left at two.'

'Out, then! All right?'

Robbie turned the volume as high as it would go and threw himself face down on his bed.

Would Carmichael say gut-wrenching was an emotion, he wondered. Because he thought so. What's more, it came in different strengths, like the OM's beer and fags.

There was the mild version, such as he'd felt that time he missed reaching Poltergeist level of *Graveyard III* by one measly decomposed skull.

Then there was the medium gut-wrench, like that caused by Daz's news about his date with Zoë Freeman.

But neither of them compared to what it felt like when the OM and his mum were arguing. Only they could produce the full-strength, health-warning, please-stop-you're-killing-me gut-wrenching he was feeling right now.

What was that poem Carmichael had made them look at on Monday? How did it start? That was it:

'How do I love thee? Let me count the ways…'

In this house? Easy. A big fat zero.

*

Robbie awoke to a truce-like silence – and thoughts of Melanie Bradshaw.

With Greg and Daz on the way, he was going to have to make a move soon. But in whose direction?

Was Mel a possible?

Would it be worth the risk?

At a tariff of ninety it would! Twilly could have made a mistake there. Robbie did the mental arithmetic, but couldn't believe the result he'd come up with. Seeing is believing. He logged the figures for good measure. He'd been right first time.

> 60-second maxi-snog with Melanie at
> 90 credits per snog-second - 60 x 90
> - 5,400 credits!

With a score like that under his belt, the *Snogathon* would be as good as his! So, he'd never really tried to get to know Micro. She'd always come across as a bit snotty-swotty. But he'd overheard her nattering to Hayley McLeod and her other mates about TV soaps and the like, so she obviously didn't spend all her time doing homework.

And she was definitely nice-looking. Pretty. Not too skinny, but not too fat either – unlike Amazon Adams, whose new tariff matched her waist measurement. OK, so she had a bit of a temper. She'd belted Daz. But if he'd been given a quid for every time he'd felt like belting Daz Hogg he'd be a rich lad by now!

No, decided Robbie, handled the right way, Mel Bradshaw probably wasn't so bad underneath. Especially underneath that blouse!

All he had to do was get to know her better.

Thursday 8th October

Greg Morris has given Hayley the push! As far as I could make out between her heartbroken sobs and snuffles, he said much as it hurt he'd decided to devote his time to getting straight As in Maths and Greed, or whatever subjects he needs to become a fat cat in the city.

Emotion: concern.

Although I've been talking to Zoë Adams more lately (especially after the Hogg incident - the other girls are now calling the pair of us 'The Heavy Mob'!), Hayley has always been my one real proggie-watching pal. And she's going to need me at this time. Who else is going to tell her what's been happening in all our favourite soaps!

Greg told them how he'd given Hayley McLeod the elbow.

'Sent her an e-mail, didn't I? Cleaner that way. No tear stains down the front of me shirt.'

'An e-mail? Saying what?'

'Heartbreaking decision, but got to dedicate self to future career. Call her when I've made my first million, shouldn't have long to wait, all my devotion.'

'To summarise, then,' said Twilly. 'Hayley is back on the market. And Daz is hoping to open his account with Zoë Freeman – when, Daz?'

'Straight after school tomorrow,' said Daz. 'I'm walking her home. St Peter's Churchyard route. Brookesie and Greg to do the tombing – I mean timing!'

*

They were behind a huge stone angel, crouching down and out of sight, with time to spare. Greg used it to good advantage.

'Time you got off the mark, isn't it, Brookesie?' he taunted. 'I was expecting you to give me more of a challenge.'

Robbie played it cool. 'Early days, Gregso. I'm playing a tactical game.'

'So am I. It's called all-out attack!'

Greg carried on talking as he poked his head round one of the angel's wings to see if Daz and Zoë were coming. 'Got anybody lined up, then?'

Mel Bradshaw. Nice healthy tariff and figure to

match. Sixty seconds with her and you won't be looking so cheery!

'You'll find out soon enough,' said Robbie, keeping his thoughts to himself. Telling Greg his plan would have been a stupid move. He hadn't even worked out a good way of telling Mel Bradshaw yet.

The arrival of Daz and Zoë Freeman brought the discussion to an abrupt end. 'Here they come!' hissed Greg, ducking back behind the angel.

Peering out cautiously, Robbie saw the pair meandering along the pathway towards them. He expected them to stop under a tree, somewhere a respectable distance away, but no. Daz had clearly forgotten where they'd agreed he and Greg should hide. He sat Zoë down on a great square slab no more than ten metres away, with the result that they got the full benefit of hearing Daz's totally original chat-up technique.

'You've got lovely eyes, Zoë. Nice colour.'

'Do you like turquoise then, Daz?'

'Er...at Christmas, yeah. Anyway, as I was saying, I like the colour of your eyes. Let's have a closer look.'

She couldn't fall for that one, thought Robbie. *Surely not even Zoë Freeman could fall for that one!*

He squinted out through a gap beneath the angel's left armpit. Wrong. Zoë was falling for that one. Daz's lips would soon be within striking distance.

'Can I kiss you, Zoë?' he oozed.

'Ooh, I don't know about that, Daz...' said Zoë, drawing back out of range.

Good on you, Zoë! thought Robbie. *Play hard to get!*

But Daz had got his chat line all ready. And what a line! It made his opening move sound brilliant.

'You see, Zoë...I only ask because, well, I've never kissed a girl before. My mum always told me I'd catch germs if I kissed anybody on the lips. She said they hide behind your tonsils and dive across the minute they get the chance. I've only just found out it wasn't true. Dad told me he had his tonsils out when he was ten and he gets 'flu every year...'

Zoë gave a stifled giggle. 'Daz, really! You don't expect me to believe that!'

'It's true! Honest!'

Whether Zoë believed it or not didn't matter. Daz had got her giggling. On he went with his mad chat, at the same time moving his big puckered lips like a cobra closing on its prey.

'Anyway, Zoë, it's left me really scared. I don't know if I'll ever be able to pluck up the courage to do it. I'm losing sleep over it...'

Three centimetres. Two centimetres...

'That's why I thought, well, I'll ask Zoë. She's the

compassionate sort, the sort who'll appreciate a boy's fears and not laugh at him, but be...'

One centimetre...

'Well, you know...understanding...'

Zero!

Robbie glanced at his watch, out beneath the angel's armpit, back to his watch again – and again, and again, until the second hand had ticked round to hit the full minute. Even at Zoë's lowly tariff of ten, Daz had well and truly got off the mark.

Within hours Twilly would be recording his credits in the *Snog Log* and turning out a revised *Snogathon* league table. And Robbie didn't need his calculator to know that it wouldn't make pleasant reading:

1.	Morris, G.	1,260
2.	Hogg, D.	600
3=	Brookes, R.	0
3=	Atwill, M.	0

He'd be in equal third place. If Twilly put their names in alphabetical order, he'd be last!

Grimly, he nodded at Greg. They slid away, out through the churchyard gates and into the High Street. Behind them, Zoë was still being understanding.

*

When Robbie pushed through the door of the Zygs' on Saturday morning, it was to have Mr Zyg bawl at him from an easy chair behind the counter.

'Robbie! You strong lad. Can you come and help for an hour one evening after school? The boss lady, she won't let me pack shelves!'

Mrs Zyg immediately came out from the store room, wagging her finger. 'I not let him pack shelves because doctor say he not pack shelves,' she called. 'He has the big blood pressure.'

'Not big,' corrected Mr Zyg with a booming laugh. 'High!'

'Big, high, same thing,' said Mrs Zyg. 'I want you dancing again. Take bloody pressure pills and you will.'

'I know, lovey,' said Mr Zyg, with a wink that only Robbie could see. 'Tell you what. We do the deal. I take pill, you give me kiss.'

'You terrible man!' Mrs Zyg squawked, even though she was looping her arms round his neck at the same time. And when she said, 'You got the deal,' it was in a different voice altogether.

Agreeing to come in for an hour after school on Wednesdays, Robbie loaded up his papers and headed out. Behind him, Mr Zyg was saying something that was funny enough – or rude enough – to make his wife giggle and kiss him at the same time.

Amazing, thought Robbie. Maybe he should develop high blood pressure if that was the effect it had on women! Something to appeal to Mel Bradshaw's softer side. He was sure Mel had one. It was just finding an excuse to get close enough to feel around for it!

Sixth Week of Term

Becoming Partners

The excuse Robbie was looking for came out of the blue. It didn't require him to catch anything contagious or to shed blood. And it came from a most unexpected quarter. None other than D. Carmichael, English teacher.

'Here's an example of good observation, mixed in with that well-known emotion called love,' he'd said, handing out a photocopied sheet. Robbie glanced at it. Another dead bit of poetry by another dead poet.

> The Passionate Shepherd to his Love
>   by Christopher Marlowe (1564–93)
>
> Come live with me, and be my love,
> And we will all the pleasures prove
> That hills and valleys, dales and fields
> And all the craggy mountains yields.
>
> There we will sit upon the rocks
> And see the shepherds feed their flocks,
> By shallow rivers to whose falls
> Melodious birds sing madrigals.

'I know it's a bit slushy,' said Carmichael. 'All right, very slushy. That's why I want you to spend a couple of weeks writing a parody of that poem.'

'A pair o' what?' Daz asked suggestively.

'Par-o-dy, Mr Hogg. It means using the same style, but in a comical or satirical way. Thus, you might write a version which begins: "Come fly with me…"'

'And be my bird,' Robbie half-yawned.

'Thank you, Mr Brookes. We may just have stumbled on an exercise suited to your peculiar talents.'

That was when Carmichael came out with it. The excuse. The good bit, the great bit, the fantastic bit.

'For this exercise I want you to work with what I call a poetry partner. The idea is that you and your partner offer each other sensible and honest criticism,' said Carmichael.

Even as Daz began leaning Robbie's way to suggest they pair up, the teacher's voice was rising a notch. 'Which means no cosy get-togethers with your best buddy. I will choose your partners for you. Nothing original, I'm afraid. Alphabetical order. So – Sandra Adams will partner Malcolm Atwill…'

In other circumstances, Robbie might have had a fleeting pang of sympathy for Twilly. But they weren't the circumstances. Because, his mind racing ahead faster than a greyhound with its tail on fire, he'd already worked out what the next pairing was going to be.

'Melanie Bradshaw will partner Robert Brookes...'

Yes! Robbie looked Mel's way. She was looking straight down at her desk. *Shy? Stunned? Not wanting to show how pleased she is? All three, probably!*

On went Carmichael, pairing them up. By the time it was over, Robbie was giving thanks for the power of the alphabet. It couldn't have worked out better if he'd decided the twosomes himself. With 'F' and 'H' being in close proximity, Daz Hogg and Zoë Freeman had got each other. No chance of a new conquest for Daz there. Best of all, with Morris following McLeod, Greg had been landed with ex-snogee and no-more-points-possible Hayley!

So for the next couple of weeks all three of his rivals were going to struggle, whereas he'd been handed on a plate the perfect excuse to approach, chat up and generally suggest getting it together with Melanie tariff-of-ninety Bradshaw.

And what better time than the present? As the lesson ended, Robbie ambled over to break the ice.

'You and me, then, Mel,' he said.

'So it seems,' she said.

Robbie winked. 'Poetry partners.'

'Oh, you were listening then?'

'I was to that bit. So...er...do you want to meet, then?'

'Definitely.'

'Great! When?'

'This time next week.'

'Not before? I'm free most nights.'

'That figures. I can't imagine anybody paying for you.'

Robbie tried being complimentary. 'Good one, Mel. Like it.'

'But will I like it, Robbie? This poem you're going to write, I mean.' Mel sighed. 'Robbie, I can hardly wait to read it.'

'In that case...'

'But I'll force myself. See you next week. Bye-ee!'

Robbie watched her go, feeling rather like he'd just been in a sword fight with one of the Three Musketeers. She was playing it cool, no doubt about that. Cool to the point of freezing, in fact. But had he made a bit of progress by the end?

I can hardly wait to see your poem, she'd said, *but I'll force myself.*

What was the saying his mum was always quoting whenever the OM claimed something insulting he'd said had only been a joke? *Many a true word is spoken in jest*, that was it.

Yes, Mel may just have let her true feelings slip there!

Monday 12th October

I just can't express how I feel.

How could you, Dave? How could you, how could you, how could you?

How could you land me with Robbie Brookes? Judging by the few words we exchanged at the end of the lesson it's going to be like expecting Dr Redrow of The Surgeon to have a sensible discussion with an inmate from the nut-house.

Emotion: despair.

*

The pattern of Robbie's evenings changed – even ignoring Wednesdays, when he'd helped out at the Zygs'.

He didn't watch the television quite as much, didn't play *Graveyard III* for quite so long, didn't stick his headphones on and belt through quite as many CDs. Instead, he started thinking about his poetry homework.

To be more accurate, he started thinking how he could use the golden chance he'd been given to come up with some verses that would get Melanie Bradshaw's pulse racing. Do that, and the *Snogathon* would swing his way. As he waited for some inspiration, he logged the current situation as he saw it.

Daz: struggling. He's already at maximum

duration with Zoë, but as well as being understanding she's got claws like a cat, so he hasn't been able to pluck up the courage to ditch her.

Greg: also in trouble. Landing Hayley as poetry partner has given him a severe handicap. Dodging her is taking all his time.

Twilly: still unattached. Says he isn't worried, the race is over three miles not five furlongs, whatever that means.

Yes, all the signs were good. Just so long as he could crack this poetry business. What had Carmichael said? A parody could be comical or satirical. But that didn't mean it couldn't contain a message, did it?

Now, what had been the bit Carmichael had been impressed with? The bit that had made him think this parody lark was right up his street? Yes, that was it:

Come fly with me, and be my bird
I'll something something, if you say the word.

Maybe he could build on that...

Come fly with me, and be my bird
I'll be on your tail if you say the word.

A bit too pushy? He tried again.

I'll be on your tail if you say the word.
I'll cheep like mad if you say the word.

Too smart.

Come fly with me, and be my bird
I'll be the happiest something that's ever been heard.

Robbie frowned. It didn't have the right feel about it.
Did big Willie have this sort of trouble turning stuff
out?
Ah! Turning! That was it. He needed to turn it round.
Make it clear that the girl was the lucky one.

Come out with me, and you'll be fine
Like a lucky person with her own gold mine.

Better!

Come out with me, and you'll be fine
Like a lucky person with her own gold mine.
A snap of my fingers is the sign...

Much better! Cool, with a hint of macho like in the

after-shave adverts. Now he was getting somewhere!

Was Melanie making just as good progress, he wondered...

*

Thursday 15th October

Emotion: apathy.

I just can't bring myself to start writing a poem to discuss with Robbie Brookes. Simple inspiration won't be enough. I'll need an anaesthetic as well.

*

For once the best part of Friday's tutor group session took place before Chesty even made her entrance.

Ambrosia Skipper climbed on a chair and announced, 'Hey, listen. You're all invited to my Hallowe'en party! Sunday of half-term week. It's going to be really cool. And dead spooky! All the windows are going to be blacked out!'

'How are we going to see what we're doing then?' shouted Greg.

'Feel our way around, of course!' hooted Daz.

A party. *It's all slotting together!* thought Robbie. If he could wow Mel Bradshaw with his poem next week, he'd be in an ideal position to ask her to the Hallowe'en party. There he'd rake in the credits – and, to pinch Carmichael's corny joke, the others wouldn't have a *ghost* of a chance of catching him!

*

Late Sunday morning Robbie wandered down, bleary-eyed, to catch the tail end of another row between the OM and his mum.

All the OM said was: 'I'll probably be late home tomorrow.'

She said, 'Again?'

'What do you mean, "again"?' he snapped.

'You were late home three times last week.'

'I've told you, I've got a big job on! Paperwork to do, phonecalls to make…'

'So how come your mobile was turned off when I tried to get you Wednesday evening?'

'How the hell do I know? Flat battery! Fault in the system! For Pete's sake, don't you trust me, woman?'

When Robbie's mum simply stared at him without answering, the OM went mental. Jumping up from the table, scattering cups as he went, he stormed out of the house.

Robbie's usual tactic when his parents had a row was to keep quiet and butt out as fast as he could. This time, he didn't. The OM needn't have stormed out. This was one bust-up that could have been avoided.

'Why couldn't you have said you trust him? Eh? What was so hard about that?'

His mum didn't answer, just gave Robbie a bitter

smile, ruffled his hair in the irritating way that made him feel he was still six years old, then padded off upstairs to get ready to face the day.

She'd muttered something to herself on the way, but Robbie hadn't heard it. Not properly, anyway, because it had sounded like, 'Because I don't trust him, that's why,' and that couldn't have been it.

*

After taking his mind off things with an extended session on *Graveyard III* (it had been a devil of a job hitting Exorcism Level, but he'd finally made it), he pulled out his Carmichael log. Flipping the pages he looked again at his most recent effort.

> Come out with me, and you'll be fine
> A snap of my fingers is the sign
> That you should follow straight away
> Like Jack and Jill we'll go out to play!

It was getting there, no question about it. What it needed was something that would get Mel Bradshaw's heart pounding at the thought of him picking her.

> ~~...That you should follow straight away~~
> ~~Like Jack and Jill we'll go out to play!~~
> That you've been picked for hours of joy

You can be my girl and I'll be your boy!

Close. Still not quite there, though. A bit too sloppy. More the sort of thing Mr Zyg would leave on Mrs Zyg's pillow.

What he needed was something with a bit more pulling power…

An OM-free Sunday lunch, an OM-present but gloweringly silent supper, and a brain-racking evening went by before he got it.

Yes!

Knock-out!

Perching his Carmichael log on his pillow, Robbie pulled out the cleanest sheet of paper he could find and began copying out his final effort.

> Come out with me, and you'll be fine
> A snap of my fingers is the sign
> That you've been picked for hours of FUN
> A date with me – you lucky one!

If that didn't get Mel Bradshaw's emotions bubbling like a cauldron then he'd be forced to conclude that she'd had them surgically removed!

*

Sunday 18th October

10.05 p.m.

I want to record, even if it is a record for my eyes only, that I'm doing this under protest. Time spent on poetry for DC is a labour of love. But writing something to show Robbie Brookes is like cooking a gourmet meal you know you're going to be tipping straight in a slop bucket.

So the only way I can cope with this, Dave, is to imagine that I'm writing it for you. No (gulp): to imagine that I'm writing it to you!

From a Passionate Disciple to Her Guru

Come be with me, my dream by day
I want you near, not far away
Then I can get to know you better
Flesh and blood, not words and letters.

Seventh Week of Term
Being a Masterful Guy to a Worried Gal

The first surprise of Monday afternoon was discovering that Carmichael had switched them from their usual room to the hall.

'Scatter to different points of the compass, please,' he called out. 'Talk about each other's verses. I'll be wandering round if you need any help.'

They scattered. Robbie watched Greg shuffle miserably behind Hayley to a spot slap-bang in the middle of the hall before sitting as far away as he could while still being in earshot. *Nice!*

He watched Daz and Zoë heading for the far corner, looking as if swapping poems was the last thing on their minds. And, in the opposite corner, he saw Twilly and Amazon Adams sitting at arm's length like a couple of strangers.

Now, where was Mel? Ah, near the stage. *Very appropriate!* Ready to give a performance of his own, Robbie grabbed a chair and headed her way.

'Hi!' he said, plonking himself down beside her.

She gave him a thin smile. He thought it was a smile.

Definitely thin, anyway. 'You want to go first?' said Robbie.

'No, you can.'

'Brains before beauty, eh? Right. Here's mine.'

Mel took his sheet of paper, gave it a glance, then sighed aloud, 'Tum-tee-tum, you'll be fine, snap of my fingers is the sign, tum-tee-tum, hours of fun, date with me you lucky one. OK, I've read it.'

'I called it "From a Masterful Guy to a Worried Gal," said Robbie.

'Good title. I can see why she's worried.'

'That clear is it?'

'Crystal. The guy's got a brain the size of a gnat.'

'Eh?'

'And the same goes for any girl dumb enough to take him up on his offer,' said Mel. She raised one eyebrow. 'Right, Robbie?'

It hadn't been the best of starts. How to play it next? *The OM's way*, he decided. Even as he sat there, an image flashed through his mind.

Last Christmas, dead boring party at their place, but as he'd sat in the corner with a mountain of crisps, there'd been the OM really turning on the charm with Gemma, one of Mum's friends. Mum hadn't looked best pleased – they'd had a row about it afterwards, real Happy Christmas stuff – but Gemma had been lapping it up, all laughs and smiles and touching the OM's arm.

Yes, the OM's way it was: don't be modest, tell 'em you're great, make 'em believe it.

In he dived.

'No way, Mel. You've got it all wrong. My guy's not dumb. He's sussed that the girl's thinking she hasn't got a chance of getting it together with him on account of how he's in such demand. So he's telling her, "Don't worry, babe. It's your lucky day. Out of the millions clamouring for my body, I've picked you. Just follow me and I'll take care of everything."'

'Oh, I see!' cried Mel. 'Big strong man looks after feeble little woman!' She gave Robbie a look like a laser beam. 'You must be joking.'

'I think you're right, Miss Bradshaw. By the sound of it Mr Brookes has written a parody that is not only comical but also tongue-in-cheek. Am I right, Mr Brookes?'

Robbie looked up. Never had he been so pleased to see Carmichael talking to him!

'Got it in one, Mr Carmichael. Joke.'

Phew. It had been a tricky moment, all right. But never let it be said that Robbie Brookes couldn't think on his feet. Or, in this case, think on his seat. He saw a way of turning the situation round – and went for it.

'What's the title of yours then, Mel?' he asked.

Mel's heart leaped, either from embarrassment or anger, she wasn't sure which. Both, probably. There she'd been, all ready to tell Bozo Brookes what he could do with his arrogant little rhyme, and now he'd put hers in the spotlight.

'Er…it hasn't got a title,' she stammered.

Well, she could hardly have said 'From a Passionate Disciple to Her Guru' when the guru was standing beside her, could she?

Robbie leaned across and plucked it from her fingers. 'You want me to read it for you, Mr Carmichael?'

'No!'

But Dave Carmichael was saying, 'Don't be modest, Miss Bradshaw. Poets have to pop their heads above the parapet. Read on, Mr Brookes.'

All Mel could do was sit there and listen as her words – her words! – were read aloud by a boy who wouldn't know what a decent poem was if she rolled it up and stuck it down his throat.

'Come be with me, my dream by day. I want you near, not far away. Then I can get to know you better. Flesh and blood, not words and letters.'

Puffin' hell, thought Robbie. *No wonder she hadn't given it a title. It was red hot!*

Maybe he should impress Carmichael and suggest a couple? 'From A Drooling Dolly to Her Mystery Man', maybe? Or 'From a Bursting Bird To her Hidden Heart-throb?'

But Carmichael was saying, 'So, Mr Brookes. Comments?'

The giblet. What could he say? Robbie scanned Mel's verse again, hoping for an idea or two.

I want you near, not far away...
Flesh and blood, not words and letters.

Suddenly, a thought struck him. A pulsating thought. He glanced at Mel. She'd gone pink. Why?

Could it be because the most spot-on title for her little effort would be something along the lines of: 'From a Shy Girl Named Mel who Tries to Give the Impression She Doesn't Care but Really Fancies Somebody in Her English Class who Just Happens to Sit on The Other Side of the Room...Somebody by the Name of Robbie Brookes'?

And Carmichael had given him the opening, so she couldn't avoid answering! He started testing the water. 'This girl – it is a from a girl, yeah?'

Good start. Mel was nodding, bashful-like. He ploughed on.

'Well, this girl's a bit of a shy one. She probably stays in a lot – y'know, reading books and watching the telly

– but every day she sees this guy. She can't believe he'd be interested in her. So she writes him letters and poems and stuff while she dreams about what it would be like if she ever did get her hands on him. How's that?'

Carmichael was nodding. 'A trifle coarse, Mr Brookes, but I'd have thought you were probably on the right track. Yes or no, Miss Bradshaw?'

Mel felt as if her lungs had run out of air. Call it luck, bad luck, but Brookes had got a bit too close to the truth. And with Dave Carmichael standing close enough for her to catch a whiff of his splash-on body lotion, she just knew her face must be looking like she'd just contracted scarlet fever with complications.

'Er...yes,' she stammered. 'K-kind of. I suppose. Yes.'

Not the smartest reply, but what else could she have done? Flung her arms round his neck and cried, 'Yes, Dave! And you're the guy in question!'

Hardly. Anyway, the crisis seemed to have passed. Over on the far side, Sandra Adams and Malcolm Atwill seemed to be having some kind of argument. With a quick, 'Excellent. Well done, both of you,' Dave Carmichael had headed over to sort it out. Yes, panic over.

Or was it? Robbie Brookes was moving his chair closer. 'You know what I'd tell this girl of yours?' he was saying. 'I'd tell her to go for it, that's what I'd tell her.'

Mel stiffened. *He can't be thinking what I think he's*

thinking – can he? That my poem is about him?

'I mean,' said Robbie, as convincingly as he could, 'if I was the guy she was pining for…well, I'd want her to stop all the faffing about and tell him straight. You know what I mean?'

He is thinking that!

'Oh you would, would you?' she said.

Robbie saw the look of surprise. Shock, more like. He couldn't blame her. He grinned. She smiled. He'd cracked it!

'I certainly would, Mel,' he said.

'Then I've got news for you, Robbie. The inspiration for my poem was the way Hayley feels about you.'

Robbie jerked back so fast he nearly suffered whiplash injuries. 'Hayley?'

Mel patted his hand. 'Hayley. She's the one who's dreaming of you, Robbie. Go for it.'

Hayley? Hayley McLeod? Well I'll be puffin' puffed.

Hayley McLeod fancied him?

No prob. With a tariff of twenty-one, it wasn't going to take much effort for him to fancy her!

*

Tuesday 20th October

    6.40 a.m.

    Emotion: guilt.

    But not about fending off Robbie Brookes with

a lie. He was coming on so strong I wouldn't have felt guilty about fending him off with a boat-hook. No, guilty about bringing Hayley into it. How could I have done that to my best friend?

Emotion: hope.

I'll admit what I've done. With luck she'll forgive me and compare it to the sort of subterfuge that Dr Redrow sometimes has to resort to when he's asked what he's doing creeping out of the nurses' hostel at two in the morning.

*

Mel's chance came at lunchtime when, after strolling slowly across the cafeteria floor, Hayley sat down beside her and asked, 'Did Greg look my way?'

'No. He was picking that spot on the side of his nose.'

Hayley looked miserable. 'He's ignoring me, Mel. I know he is. I hoped he would get fed up with his share prices and come back to me, but he hasn't.'

The mention of boys had been the opening Mel needed to make her confession. But with Hayley now picking at her lunch like a sad sparrow, she decided that it might be best if she tried to cheer her up first. And it worked – but not in the way she'd intended.

'I think you should forget Greg Morris, Hay. There are other fish in the sea.'

'I don't want a fish. I want Greg.'

Mel put an arm round her friend's shoulders. 'I understand that, but, well...if Greg Morris isn't interested in you, then I know somebody else who is.'

'Somebody else? Who?'

'Robbie Brookes...'

Mel waited for Hayley to cackle like a witch at the very idea. That's what she'd expected her to do. She'd then expected that they'd have a huge laugh, she'd admit what she'd told Brookes at the poetry partner session, they'd both have another good laugh, and that would be that.

Only...Hayley hadn't cackled like a witch. Instead, a smile had crossed her face as if it was the sun coming out.

'Really? Robbie Brookes? Robbie Brookes fancies me? How do you know?'

Tuesday 20th October

  9.55 p.m.

  Emotion: guilt again!

Hayley looked so happy when I told her Robbie Brookes fancied her that I just got carried away. Digging in my bag and giving her his big-headed 'From a Masterful Guy to a Worried Gal' poem just seemed to happen. So did me saying: read that, Hay, Robbie said you were his inspiration.

No! she said. Then she read it, eyes widening by the line. Yes! she said.

Who knows where it will all lead? There's one consolation, though. Hayley's definitely forgotten about Greg Morris!

*

Twilly opened his briefcase, laid the *Snog Log* carefully on Mrs Zyg's freshly wiped table, laid his fountain pen by its side, cleared his throat and brought the extraordinary *Snogathon* meeting to order.

'I propose a special rule to cover this Hallowe'en party,' he said.

Not for the first time, Robbie wondered why Twilly was taking the whole thing quite as seriously as he was. Then he remembered the hundred-quid prize and wondered no more.

'Given that Ambrosia has invited virtually the whole of the year,' Twilly went on, 'I anticipate a number of *Snogathon* scoring opportunities – opportunities that may well arise for more than one of us at the same time.'

'You mean there could be times when we've got a bird in the hand and two in the bushes!' hooted Daz.

'In a manner of speaking,' said Twilly, solemnly. 'Which could make the two-witness rule difficult to follow. So my proposal is that, for the Hallowe'en party only, we allow scores to be verified by just a single witness. Agreed?'

'Fine by me,' said Greg.

'And me,' said Robbie.

It would make life a lot easier. If this party was going to take place in a house as dark and creepy as Ambrosia Skipper was promising, finding one witness for his anticipated snogful encounter with Hayley would be hard enough.

'How about you, Daz?'

'He won't need a witness,' said Greg. 'He's at maximum with Zoë, remember.'

'Except that,' said Daz with relish, 'I won't be going with Zoë. She's grounded. Making malicious telephone calls.'

Robbie whistled. 'Yeah? Doesn't sound like the sort of thing she'd do.'

'Well, that's what her mum called it. Zoë was only trying to help. When her mum said her new boyfriend's car wouldn't start so he was going to have to stay the night, ho-ho, what does Zoë do? Call the breakdown van! It turns up in the middle of the night, the boyfriend has to go out in his bare feet to see them and doesn't come back, Zoë's mum goes ballistic and grounds her for the rest of the term. So that's that. End of the Daz and Zoë combo. I'm back in the market, boys!'

*

It looked to Robbie as if Mr Zyg was grounded too.

Mr Zyg hadn't been too mobile during their meeting, but when he called in to do some extra shelf-packing after school had broken up on Friday, it was to find a determined Mrs Zyg hardly allowing her husband to move from his chair behind the counter. Every time he jumped up and tried to serve anybody she dashed over and beat him to it.

'I am not the invalid!' he yelled, and started pulling a box out of the storeroom to prove it. But he soon got out of breath and had to take a rest anyway.

'See,' Mrs Zyg said, 'the doctor knows. Take it easy, he says. Not take it easy and look at you.'

'OK,' he grunted, 'I will be the invalid...'

He waited for Mrs Zyg to fold her arms round his neck and give him a kiss, before booming, 'But only for today!'

She laughed, but it was a sad one. Even Robbie could tell that Mr Zyg was kidding himself.

*

Robbie spent much of the weekend trying to decide whether to ring Hayley and invite her to go to the Hallowe'en party with him or wait until he got there and make his move then.

In the end he tried logging the fors and againsts to

see if it would help. There weren't many:

For ringing: Hayley will have all week to work herself up into a state of fevered anticipation.

Against ringing: Hayley will have all week to mope around thinking I don't even know she exists so that when I waltz over to her at the party she'll be so relieved she'll throw herself at my feet in gratitude and relief.

It didn't help. He decided not to decide. There was a week to go, after all.

Half-Term Week
Finding the Bottle

It took a couple of days, but in the end the argument for ringing beat the argument against ringing. Robbie called Hayley on Tuesday...

Tuesday 27th October

Hayley phoned. Mel! You were right! Robbie Brookes has just called and asked if he could take me to the Hallowe'en party!

Emotion: guilt expunged! (if that's the right word).

Great stuff, Hay.

Trouble is, Darren Hogg had already called and asked if he could take me. Tricky one! Took me a minute to think what to do. But I sorted it out, Mel. I rang them both and told them they couldn't take me, I'd see them there.

Quick thinking. Dr Redrow couldn't have done better! They didn't argue, then?

Nah. I said I'd promised to go with you because you didn't have anyone else.

Thanks, Hay. Thanks a lot!

Hayley had sounded surprised to get his call all right! The line couldn't have gone more quiet if she'd fainted on him. Even when she did find her voice she sounded stunned – which was presumably why she didn't agree straight away but said she'd get back to him.

When she did, it was to say she'd see him at the party. *Can't blame her for that,* Robbie thought. After her bus-stop disaster with Greg she was probably playing safe and getting a lift there!

The call got him thinking, though. Having some *Snogathon* points in the bag was all very well but, he'd just realised, there were other things to be considered.

Comparisons, for a start. Like those Greg and Daz had made. Having them draw first blood had been bad enough, but sitting through their comparisons had been even worse.

'Hayley's a seven-out-of-ten snogger, lads,' had been Greg's verdict. 'A bit on the tight-lipped side, but quite sweet-tasting.'

'Sure that wasn't the popcorn?' had been all Robbie could growl in reply.

Daz had been a high marker. 'Zoë's an eight at least. Nine when she gets going with that tongue! Like snogging a pneumatic marshmallow, it is...'

Robbie was starting to worry. It was all right for the lads to make comparisons like that, but what if the babes did it as well? What if Hayley was the sort who kept a diary littered with performance figures? What if, while they were in a clinch, her mind was more on what snog-rating to give him compared to Greg?

Still fretting, he drifted off upstairs and into his room. *Technique*, he thought as he flopped his head onto his pillow. That was what separated the men from the boys – or, in his case, the Morrises from the Brookeses.

He stood up, bringing his pillow with him. Technique...

Easing one arm round the lower part of the pillow, he tried imagining it was Hayley's waist. Slowly he snaked the other arm round the pillow's top, his eyes smouldering – he hoped – like a bonfire on Guy Fawkes' night. Pulling it close, he moved in for the kill.

But even as his burning lips descended onto his fluffed-up all-sponge Hayley substitute, another thought was intruding. Timing. Wouldn't it help if he could keep time as well? To equal Greg, he too needed to hit the sixty seconds maximum. It would be gutting to lose credits by lifting off a couple of seconds early. He started counting in his head.

Elephant one, elephant two, elephant three...

He got as far as *elephant thirty* then had to come up for breath. Useless! He had to last longer. How? Take a deep breath first, he supposed. He tried again.

Elephant one, elephant two...

Yes! He was well away.

Elephant fifty-eight, elephant fifty-nine...

Technique perfected! That was the way to do it!

It was also, Robbie was about to discover, the way a pair of fully engrossed snoggers like Greg and Hayley could fail to hear a squeaky bus draw up right next to them. Because it was only after he'd hit a triumphant *elephant eighty!* and was releasing his pillow with a couple of tender pecks that he realised a phone was trilling a silly tune.

The OM's mobile. A power-shower whine told Robbie where he was, and a quick look down at the hall table told him the phone wasn't in the shower with him. Robbie hopped down the stairs and picked it up.

'Vince?' said the caller. 'It's Gemma.'

'I'm sorry, he's not available right now,' said Robbie like a teenage answering machine. 'This is his son. Can I take a message?'

'Er. Oh. No, no message. Thanks. Bye.'

*

Robbie forgot about the phonecall until, as he was putting the finishing touches to his Hallowe'en outfit, he heard the loose floorboard creak on the landing. He called out and the OM strolled in.

'Hello?' he said, then noticed what Robbie was up to. 'What you doing, kid?'

'Sewing.'

His voice rose a notch. 'Sewing! Sewing what?'

'A shroud. It's what they wrap corpses in. It's my costume for the Hallowe'en party on Saturday.'

'Yeah, but – sewing. That's what your mother's here for, kid.' Suspiciously, he fingered the greying linen sheet Robbie had found in the loft. 'What you going as then?'

'A corpse, Dad!'

It had been a bit of a brainwave, inspired by a marathon session on *Graveyard III*. Babes liked a good scream, it was a well-known biological fact. So that was going to be his tactic. He was going to leave all the others to do the usual Dracula and Frankenstein impersonations. He was going to cause a sensation as one of the risen dead! A tailored shroud, hardened green play-dough on his hands as flaking flesh and a skeleton mask would do the job nicely. He'd get Hayley's lungs wobbling like a pair of bouncy castles, then whip off his mask quick and wait for her to fall into his arms.

He just hoped she was going to be quicker than the OM. 'A corpse?' he was murmuring, 'what kind of corpse?'

'A dead one, Dad!'

Robbie decided to change the subject. Remembering the phonecall gave him the chance to do it.

'Hey, I forgot. There was a call on your mobile earlier. While you were in the shower. Somebody called Gemma.'

'Gemma?'

'Yeah. She didn't leave a message.'

'Right. Thanks.' The OM sort of frowned, then said quickly, 'Probably wants me to have a look at her car again. Women, eh? Useless. Can't change a light bulb, half of them.'

That's when it sank in. Gemma. His mum's friend, Gemma. Laughing, giggling, arm-touching-at-their-Christmas-party Gemma.

And Robbie couldn't escape the feeling that if the OM had asked him at that moment if he trusted him then he'd have had as hard a job saying yes as his mum.

*

Saturday 31st October.

Ambrosia Skipper's Hallowe'en Party

I know why it happened.

I know how it happened.

Emotion: no regrets. Not one.

Just as Robbie expected, Greg went to the party as

Dracula. He'd got hold of a black cloak and a dinner suit. His fake teeth were a bit wobbly but that didn't seem to worry him.

'By the time the babes get close enough to notice, it'll be too late!' he leered.

'Same goes for my neck bolt,' said Daz, in the guise of Frankenstein's Monster. The neck bolt was on a wire hoop, and Daz had given himself multiple scars round his wrists and across his throat. He'd got himself an ugly rubber mask, so it gave Robbie a good laugh when Ambrosia Skipper opened the front door and trilled, 'Hi, everybody, Hi, Darren!'

As for Twilly – if ever he turned his mind to crime, thought Robbie, the police were going to have their work cut out. He'd thought about things...and turned up as a Recording Angel.

'Perfect excuse for carrying a *Snogathon* credit-scoring pencil and notepad,' he whispered.

Robbie couldn't argue with that. It was inspired planning, all right, even if Twilly did look a total dongle in his white sheet and tinsel halo. His own outfit, however, was going to cause him an immediate problem.

Ambrosia's parents had indeed allowed her to turn the place into a haunted house. All the lounge windows had been black-curtained. It was like being in a coalmine with a bag over his head until his eyes started to get used to it; then it was like being in a coalmine *without* a bag over his head.

Useless. He could be hitting the high spots with Hayley in the middle of the floor and an observer wouldn't be able to tell. That was assuming he could see enough to find her in the first place. It seemed to be a bit brighter at the far end of the room, so he groped his way in that direction.

The light turned out to be the entrance to the food and drink area. The end part of the Skippers' L-shaped lounge, it had been done up like a witch's den and divided off from the main party area by a curtain of clinging black gauze acting as pretend cobwebs. More importantly, there inside was Hayley, nattering to Ambrosia and Melanie.

Robbie started to push his way through the gauze towards them, only to discover what tricky stuff gauze was. Surprisingly clingy. Especially to hands and arms and a skeleton mask coated in hardened green play-dough. Before he knew it, the gauze was catching on him left, right and centre, so that when Robbie finally popped out of the other side it was like a ghostly version of Halley's Comet trailing a cloud of green play-dough.

Worse, by then Hayley and Co. had gone out the other way – and house-proud Mrs Skipper, carrying an expensive-looking punch bowl, had come in.

It was a short discussion, Robbie remembered, and very one-sided. Basically, he'd said nothing while she'd screeched something along the lines of 'I'm not having you tread that stuff in my carpets get in the bathroom and scrape it off this instant or you'll be out on your ear friend of Ambrosia's or no friend of Ambrosia's!'

So off he'd trekked upstairs to spend half an hour peeling himself like he was a human puffin' grape only to discover, when he finally came down again, that loads of people had disappeared.

Hayley McLeod and Darren Hogg, to name just two...

They hadn't long been gone.

After leaving the eating area, Mel and Hayley had jigged around for a while in the lounge until out of the darkness had stepped Darren Hogg, flashing a torch.

'Hayley, baby!'

'Daz!' cried Hayley. 'I was wondering if you'd find me in the dark!'

Daz landed a scarred wrist on her shoulder and started whispering in her ear like he was crooning into a microphone.

Mel had been all ready to leave them to it when Hayley suddenly grabbed her elbow. 'Melanie! We're off!'

'We've only just got here, Hay. My mother's hardly had time to start worrying.'

'Not home. Off out. We're going trick-or-treating! A load of us. Just down the road and round the corner. Come on!'

Mel went, if only because it was lighter out in the street and she quite fancied seeing the back of her hands again. Which was how she came to be among the heaving group of ugliness which roared out into the dark, dark night and saw what it did...

One who hadn't disappeared, Robbie soon discovered, was Ambrosia Skipper. As he drifted into the food and drinks area she and Mrs Skipper were on either side of the kitchen table, arguing. In between them was the punch bowl he'd seen Mrs Skipper carrying earlier. Then it had been empty, but now it was sloshing with an orange-coloured mixture and floating fruit topping. That seemed to be the topic under discussion.

'Ambrosia,' Mrs Skipper was saying firmly, 'I don't care if your encyclopaedia does say that a punch isn't a punch unless it's got five ingredients, one of which must be seriously alcoholic, this punch is having nothing stronger in it than fruit juice!'

'But, Mum...'

'No, Ambrosia. N. O. No!'

Making clear that that was her final word, Mrs Skipper stalked off. Behind her, Ambrosia was looking like she'd swallowed a whole lemon. Then she saw Robbie and her face lit up like she was lost in the desert and he was an oasis.

'Robbie! Just the person I need!'

'Yeah?'

'Definitely.' And, with that, Ambrosia rummaged around in the folds of her witch's gown and whipped out the bottle of vodka she'd filched from the cocktail cabinet. 'Empty this in the bowl for me.'

'Me?'

'Yes, you. That way, if Mummy finds out and asks me if I did it, I can say no with a clear conscience!'

Robbie hesitated. At least he did until Ambrosia placed her hand on his arm and murmured, 'I'll be ever so grateful, Robbie.'

Grateful! Without a second thought, Robbie grabbed the bottle and emptied it into the punch bowl. Ambrosia stirred the vodka in with a posh glass ladle, then scooped out two glassfuls.

Still looks like an orangey squash, thought Robbie, *but, puffin' hell, it doesn't taste like it!*

The first sip felt like molten lava coursing down his throat. So did the next two or three. But by the time he'd refilled his glass a couple of times, he was definitely getting used to it.

'Now where shall we go?' purred Ambrosia, taking his arm. 'I know. The garden.'

Wa-hey! It was Ambrosia-the-Grateful time!

Except that...he needed an observer! If they'd all gone off with the others he was sunk. So it was with great delight that he saw, plunging through the gauze and into the room, none other than Twilly the Recording Angel himself! Robbie just had time to stick a thumb in the air as a sign for him to follow before Ambrosia dragged him outside.

Not just outside the back door, either. Much further. Down a winding stone path, across the grass, and round behind a towering fir tree.

'This should do,' said Ambrosia.

Robbie couldn't have agreed more! He slid an arm round her shoulders, hoping she would automatically melt into pillow position. She didn't. What she did instead was to lob the empty vodka bottle into the middle of the fir tree with a cackle and a cry of 'My stingy mother will never find it in there!'

She wanted to come down here to hide the evidence? That's all? That's puffin' all?!

It certainly looked that way. Ambrosia was making to head off back up towards the house – just as a flash of Recording Angel white told him that Twilly was in the act of creeping into position on the other side of the tree.

'Ambrosia!' squawked Robbie. 'Hang on. We've, er…only just got here.'

His arm was still round her shoulders. What he needed now was to get her head tilted upwards, pillow-position. He did the only thing he could think of and pointed up at the clear night sky with his free hand while tightening his grip with the other.

'It's stopped peeing down, then,' he said.

It could have been a smoother line, he knew. But that wasn't what caused the problem. It was drawing Ambrosia's attention to the heavens. Unwittingly, he'd triggered off a classic Ambrosia Skipper babble bout.

'Oh, look at all those stars, Robbie. Billions and billions of them. Do you know, I read in the paper the other day that somebody had done a survey and found that twenty-two per cent of young people definitely believe in aliens and thirty-nine per cent think there's probably something out there somewhere.'

Her head was tilted at the perfect angle. His arm was round her. If only she'd belt up, he was there.

'You know what I think?' said Ambrosia, doing anything but belt up. 'I think I don't know what to think, really I don't. I mean, with all those billions and billions of stars and solar systems and stuff I suppose they're right when they say the chances of our planet being the only one with life on it are unimaginably small.'

Unlike your mouth, Ambrosia!

On she went. 'But then I say to myself: what about paperclips? And corks? And bottle-tops?'

Robbie didn't know what she was on about, but the mention of corks suggested the only way he was going to get anywhere before Twilly's five-year watch battery went flat. Sliding his spare arm round her waist, he puckered up and zoomed in. It was like trying to hit a moving target.

'I mean, there must be billions and billions of paperclips in the world, mustn't there...' Ambrosia said, still nattering on even as he was trying to land a good one.

Yes! Elephant one, elephant two...

'...and corks...'

Elephant three, elephant four, elephant five...

'...and bottle-tops. So the likelihood of that vodka bottle-top ending up here...'

Elephant six, elephant seven...

'...is also unimaginably small...'

Elephant eight, elephant nine, elephant ten!

That would just have to do, decided Robbie. Dodge about any more and he'd end up with a ricked neck.

'But it did happen, didn't it?' said Ambrosia.

'Yeah, I think so,' he growled.

'Ambrosia!' came a screech from the house.

Ambrosia's mum, unmistakably. As she hurtled off, Robbie stayed put. If Mrs Skipper had discovered her vodka stocks were down by a bottle, then it was going to be best for him to stay out of sight. With one yellow card already, he'd definitely be turfed out for two bookable offences. Besides, he wanted to confirm his score with Twilly, who was already inching round to his side of the tree.

'Ten seconds, I made it,' he said.

Twilly shook his head. 'Three.'

'Three! You're joking! It must have been longer. She went through a complete alien probability theory.'

'That's the whole point,' said Twilly. 'Every time I started the watch I had to stop it again. You weren't in contact for more than three seconds at a time.'

'Oh, come on,' pleaded Robbie. 'Have a heart, Twilly...'

Twilly shook his head. 'Three seconds,' he said, writing in the *Snog Log*. 'At a tariff of fifteen. The judge's decision is final.'

A miserable forty-five credits. Hardly worth the damage to his eardrums. Wandering back up to the house, Robbie found himself alone in the kitchen – well, just him and the punch bowl. One or six glasses later, he wasn't sure exactly how many, he wandered back out into the garden to have another crack at persuading Twilly to see sense.

The Recording Angel was still down by the tree. Except that he seemed to be...dancing! Definitely moving from side to side, anyway. But then, so was the tree! And the grass. Robbie was still trying to work all this out when he heard the sound of footsteps behind him and felt a hand slip into his.

'Now then, where were we?' said Ambrosia, leading him to a garden seat and throwing her arms round his neck...

Rather like Robbie, Mel felt as though she'd been spending a lot of time being led from one place to another – in her case, by Darren Hogg. It was he who'd gone on in front, hammering on doors while the rest of the trick-or-treat party had loitered at front gates looking like a seething mob waiting for a reason to riot.

By the time they reached the far end of the road from Ambrosia's house they'd collected a stack of chocolate bars and £4.73 in loose change.

Hayley, acting as bounty holder, was impressed. 'It's the way Daz says "trick or treat", I reckon.'

'Or because he's actually saying "*kick* or treat",' said Mel.

Up ahead, arm waving like a hooligan majorette, Daz was leading them away from the road they'd been following and off down another that looked quite different. The road Ambrosia Skipper lived in was quite classy, with large, bow-windowed houses and more security lights than a prison. This one was decidely inferior, a street of small terraced houses.

Daz called a halt outside one with a wheelie-bin standing like a sentry beside the front door. But this time, instead of goose-stepping down the path himself, he turned to Mel and Hayley.

'Your turn, girls!' he honked.

Mel didn't move. Neither did Hayley, at first. But when the others joined in the chorus, she cracked.

'Come on, Mel,' she said. 'Girl-power. Let's show them we're their equals.'

'I don't want to be their equals, Hay. I want to stay the way I am – superior.'

'Chicken in every respect, you mean,' sneered Greg Morris, his Dracula-teeth glinting under the street lights.

The jibe hit home with Hayley. Giving Greg the kind of glare only a girl who's been dumped can give the dumper, she adjusted the horns of the red devil outfit she was wearing, swung her tail in a menacing arc, and kicked open the gate.

'Are you coming, Mel? Or do I have to do this alone?'

Mel followed – not that she had much choice. The whole gang had moved up behind them, shoving her in the back and giving a whole new meaning to the term *peer pressure.*

In the dark, Hayley couldn't find a bell push, so she ended up rattling loudly on the knocker. The whole place was so bleak and spooky Mel was almost expecting the sound to echo repeatedly before the door was finally opened with a creak by a gravel-voiced butler. But it didn't, and it wasn't. A single knock was enough to have the door opening within seconds. Not at the hands of a butler, either, but by an unshaven and scruffy man in a different profession altogether.

The teaching profession.

They'd called at Dave Carmichael's house.

Mel had to check a couple of times to make sure it really was him. He looked so different. No cool shirt, no smooth jeans, no trendy moccasins. In their place was a grubby tee, a pair of shapeless chinos and bare feet. What was more, his face matched his clothes. He hadn't combed his hair, his eyes were dark and sunken and he looked like he hadn't shaved since they'd broken up for half-term.

'Yes?' he snapped. 'What do you want?'

Mel stepped back into the shadows. She didn't want

him to recognise her. She didn't want him to know she'd recognised him, either. She reached out to drag Hayley away – but too late.

'Trick or...or...' Hayley had already begun to squawk, before drying up as she suddenly realised who she was talking to. The only consolation was that at least she had dried up and not giggled, "Ooh, hello! I didn't know you lived here!"

Mel waited for a smile, a witty quote, something clever and up-market anyway. But Dave Carmichael didn't smile, he glared.

And he didn't quote. He swore, told them they were demanding money with menaces, threatened to call the police, then swore at them again. The bitter smell from his breath still reached Mel even though she'd taken an involuntary couple of steps back as Carmichael had let rip. He was drunk.

Mel felt betrayed. Mr Dave Carmichael was a hypocrite. His school image was a sham. By accident they'd scratched his surface and revealed the real person beneath: somebody about as sensitive and artistic as a wart-hog.

She was ready to tell him so, but their teacher was taking a threatening step towards them and bawling, 'Clear off, whoever you are!'

Whoever you are? That's when it sank in. In their

Hallowe'en disguises – she with black make-up and black floppy hat covering her eyes and Hayley the red devil looking like a feverish beetroot – Carmichael hadn't recognised them.

So Mel bit her tongue – and ran. Speeding out of the front gate, they were well down the road by the time they heard his front door slam shut. And, for once, she couldn't fault Hayley's summary of the situation. 'Very poetic,' she said. 'Not.'

All the way back to Ambrosia's, Mel grew angrier and angrier. While Hayley revelled in recounting what had happened, she could think only of what she now wished she'd stayed and told Carmichael.

You're a hypocrite, Mr Dave Carmichael. A stinking hypocrite. I thought you were different. Mature and sensitive, not like the Robbie Brookeses of this world. But you're not. You're just a boozing, swearing, big boy. A typical male, crude and rude. And I hate you!

Her feelings still bubbling like a boiling kettle as they reached Ambrosia's front door, Mel made a beeline for the kitchen and something to eat. Food, that's what she needed.

What she definitely, certainly didn't need was Robbie Brookes wobbling in from the garden like a pump-up doll with a slow puncture and slurring, 'Melly-baby! Where you been all evening?...'

Robbie was feeling good. Light-headed. More than light-headed, in fact, and very, very good. Things were a bit blurry, but not so blurry that he couldn't remember what had happened after Ambrosia Skipper had grabbed him.

'My misery of a mother says I should be mixing more,' she'd snapped. 'She says I'm not being a very good hostess. She says I should be giving my guests some personal attention. So for once I'm going to do just what the old bat wants.'

And with that she'd grabbed his neck like she was an all-in wrestler, yanked his head towards hers and...

Elephant one, elephant two, elephant three, elephant four...

Even through the increasing punch-haze he'd been aware of her lips attached to his like they were suction pads and her fingers roaring up and down his spine as if it was a keyboard and she was playing *The Flight of the Bumble Bee*. It had been like snogging with an octopus.

Then, as suddenly as it had started, it had been all over. With the sounds of shouting and whooping telling her the trick-or-treating party had come back, Ambrosia had released him from her grip and raced off back up to the house.

What had happened then? Oh, yes, Twilly had come out of hiding as he'd been shaking his head and wondering if he'd been imagining things.

'Di' you see that, Twilly?' he'd asked.

'I did. Twenty seconds.'

'Twen'y seconds? Ree-lly?'

'On the dot,' Twilly had said. 'Multipled by a tariff of fifteen gives you three hundred credits.'

'Three hudren...hun'red credits! That's more like it!'

This called for a celebration. Another glass or five of that lovely tasty drinky stuff he'd helped make. Robbie headed straight – well, as straight as he could manage – back to the kitchen.

Boo. The punch bowl was nearly empty. Lots of soggy fruit and just a drain of liquid in the bottom. But who was that standing next to it, all on her ownsome, like a curvy consolation prize...

'Melly-baby! Where you been all evening?'

'Avoiding you,' snapped Mel.

Robbie blinked. 'Avoiding me? I don' believe that, Micro – I mean, Melanie. Me and you are poddery pardners, 'en we? You wouldn't wan' to 'void your poddery pardner, would you? Have a punch a glass. Did I say punch a glass? Just testin'. I mean glass a punch, course.'

Picking up the ladle, Robbie rattled it around in the

punch bowl as if he was stirring custard.

'I mean,' he burbled on, 'you're my pal, Melly. You read my li'l old poem, din' you? An' I read yours.'

He's drunk! realised Mel. *First Carmichael, now him. Teacher and pupil. Boys together!*

'You can still remember our poems, then?' she replied acidly, wanting to walk away but finding that her tongue wouldn't let her.

'Course I can remem'er them,' answered Robbie. 'Bits of 'em. "I wan' you near, not far 'way", tha's what yours said. "Then I can getta know you bedder." Right?'

'Close.'

That's impressed her! thought Robbie through the fog. He leaned closer, wagging his finger.

'An' you tol' me tha's what Hayley thought 'bout me, din' you? An' I rang her up. An' she said she'd see me at this 'ere pardy. But she hasn't. An' I haven't. So now I'm thinkin' you was tellin' me porkies, Melly. That was'n a poem 'bout Hayley's 'motions at all. I think it was 'bout somebody else's 'motions.'

'Really? Whose?'

'Yours, Melly-baby. I thin' it's you who wan's to getta know me bedder. I thin' you fancy me.'

Mel hooted. 'Fancy you? Robbie Brookes, I wouldn't fancy you if you were the last jam fancy in the fancy shop!' *And if you so much as take a step nearer, I'll tip that punch bowl over your head.*

'There you go, you're doin' it again. Pretendin' not to like me. Bud I can tell you do really. Really, really, really, really...'

She's still playing hard to get, thought the befuddled Robbie. *Only one thing to do. Actions speak louder than words, and all that. Do what Ambrosia the octopus had done to him. Get closer.*

He moved a step nearer. He paused. The punch bowl. It was levitating! Clever! How was it doing that? Oh, nothing magical. Micro Mel was lifting it up.

Why's she doing that? Hello, she's bringing it my way. Fair enough, filling up glasses takes time anyway. I'll drink it straight from the bowl. Hang on, what's she doing? She's not. She isn't. Is she? She is!

With a grace and style Chesty Weston would have applauded in a member of her netball class, Mel flipped the punch bowl over and slam-dunked it onto Robbie's head. It did the trick. The shock of soggy oranges and lemons cascading over his head and all down his front slowed his advance – and the sight of a Mrs Skipper bursting into the kitchen with her eyes popping stopped it altogether.

The sight calmed Mel, too. To her own surprise she realised her conscience wouldn't let her leave him to be torn to shreds by a rabid Mrs Skipper, or even to be laughed at by the others who were now crowding in to see what the fuss was all about.

'I'm so sorry, Mrs Skipper. It was all my fault. I was trying to tip the bowl up to get the last few drops out. Such a delicious recipe, I wish my mother was as clever. Anyway, before I knew it your beautiful bowl had slipped from my fingers.'

'Onto this idiot's head?'

'Only because Robbie saw it falling from the table and dived down to save it. He ended up an unfortunate victim.'

Trying desperately not to giggle, she reached over and plucked a wedge of orange peel from his hair. 'I *am* sorry, Robbie. Can you forgive me?'

It was the most convincing lie Robbie had ever heard in his life. Much as he could have cheerfully wrung her neck, Mel had at least given him a way out which saved him from looking a complete prawn in front of the others.

'It's cool,' he said, grateful to discover that his tongue seemed a bit more under control. 'Just bad luck. The way the cookie grumbles.'

It did the trick. Mrs Skipper almost smiled. 'Well, thank you anyway.'

Robbie waved a hand. 'No prob. Worth a lot is it, the old bowl?'

'Good heavens, no! I picked it up at a jumble sale for a pound. I wouldn't bring out anything decent with you lot around. But it would have taken ages to pick up the broken glass. So, thank you for that. Now, I think you'd better get cleaned up.'

Off went Robbie for his second trip to the bathroom. But at least when he came out this time it wasn't to find the place half empty. From below he could hear the unmistakable sounds of a party in full swing. Down the stairs he went – only to bump into somebody sitting on the bottom step.

'Hello, Robbie. I did say I'd see you here, didn't I? And – well, I've a confession to make. I said the same to somebody else. But I don't like him as much as I like you, Robbie. He doesn't go around sacrificing himself to do good deeds for my best friend.'

She patted the small square of stair carpet next to her red legs. 'Sit down, Robbie.'

'Sure thing, Hayley,' he said, as a Recording Angel hovered conveniently into position.

Eighth Week of Term
Getting the Elbow

Carmichael was the talk of the school! Hayley had been telling everybody about him looking like a drop-out and yelling obscenities at her and Mel Bradshaw.

Obscenities? considered Robbie. *Could it be that under Carmichael's wimpish exterior there lived a normal bloke? One of the lads?*

The thought was so mind-bogglingly impressive that, apart from a bit at the end when Carmichael said he was taking them on a trip out of school next week, Robbie didn't listen to a word of his lesson!

*

But at the Zygs' place, straight after school, he was all ears. Even so, Twilly had to repeat himself twice. According to the Recording Angel he, Robbie, in a stair-snogging-inspired grand gesture, had asked Hayley out. To the flicks? No. For a slap-up meal at the Zygs'!

Twilly recounted his final punch-fuelled words. 'Posh place it is. I'm so well known there, I've got a regular table.'

Ah well, maybe she wouldn't remember the details. He certainly didn't! But what he did know was that he was well and truly off the mark, *Snogathon*-wise. As Twilly opened the official *Snog Log* he sat back to await the good news that he'd rocketed up the charts.

'Brookesie and Ambrosia Skipper,' began Twilly. 'Twenty seconds. At a tariff of fifteen, equals three hundred credits.'

Robbie glanced round the table. Daz shrugged. Greg sniffed. Twilly, the hint of a smile on his face, reported on. 'Ambrosia Skipper and Malcolm Atwill: twenty seconds.'

'You?' gawped Robbie.

Twilly smiled. 'Remember she said her mum had told her to give her guests some personal attention? Well I was next on her list. Greg and Daz witnessed. Then I did the same for them.'

'Not...'

Twilly turned back to the *Snog Log* and read, 'Greg and Ambrosia Skipper, twenty seconds. Daz and Ambrosia Skipper, twenty seconds.'

Precisely twenty seconds each? Puffin' hell, Ambrosia must have been born with a clockwork brain as well as a clockwork tongue!

'So three hundred credits to all four of us,' said Twilly. 'Next, Daz and Hayley McLeod. Fourteen seconds. Two hundred and ninety-four credits.'

'What?' goggled Robbie.

Daz winked. 'Gave her an extra share of the goodies we'd collected from trick-or-treating, didn't I? It did the trick, 'cos next thing I know she's giving me a treat! I'd have done even better if she hadn't hopped off to the loo and come back to find me getting my ration from Ambrosia.'

He leaned across the table and tapped the *Snog Log* with a thick index finger. 'And talking of Ambrosia, you'd better check your records, Twilly. I did better than you lot.'

Twilly was unperturbed. 'I was coming to that. Daz and Ambrosia, part two. Daz improves personal best to thirty-four seconds. Five hundred and ten credits.'

'How'd you manage that?' squawked Greg.

'Last one in her attention-giving queue, wasn't I?' grinned Daz. 'She didn't have anyone else to go to! So while I was at it I asked her out. Maximum Ambrosia-credits as good as in the bag!'

'Next,' said Twilly. 'Greg and Purity Meek. Seventeen seconds.'

Greg explained with relish. 'Asked if the Dracula teeth were real, didn't she? "Only one way to find out, darling," I said, and started on her neck. Worked me way up from there!'

'At a tariff of eighteen makes three hundred and six credits,' droned Twilly.

'More on the way there as well,' gloated Greg. 'I'm going out with Purity now.'

'Finally,' said Twilly, 'Brookesie and Hayley...'

Daz pointed a laughing finger. 'So that's where she went after me!'

'...Thirty-nine seconds,' announced Twilly, shutting Daz up nicely, 'at a tariff of twenty-one, makes eight hundred and nineteen credits.'

His fingers darted over the buttons of his calculator, he scribbled a few more figures in the *Snog Log*, then turned it so they could all see the current position. Robbie viewed the figures without joy.

1. Morris, G.	1,866
2. Hogg, D.	1,404
3. Brookes, R.	1,119
4. Atwill, M.	300

Still only in puffin' third place! But – there was hope, wasn't there? Twilly was lagging badly and both Greg and Daz were lined up with babes on much lower tariffs than Hayley. His spirits lifted. Maybe the situation wasn't so bad!

Twilly – he was the one he couldn't make out. After pushing so hard to make the *Snogathon* happen, it seemed like he was hardly trying to win. Odd.

Robbie pushed the thought to the back of his mind. What he had to do now was concentrate on working his way up the table with Hayley. Their dinner date would be a chance to do just that – so long as Mrs Zyg's microwaved pasties didn't let him down!

Monday 2nd November
English lesson taken by a nonentity, an educational pygmy. I am withdrawing my labour at this subject, anyway. With luck by the end of term my work will be so appalling I'll be banished to the noggins' group and will never have to suffer one of Dave the fraud Carmichael's lessons ever again.

Tuesday 3rd November
Saw Mr creep Carmichael at the vending machine. Didn't give him a second look, and may the chicken sandwich he bought be riddled with salmonella and make him spontaneously overflow with a dose of powerful trots.

Sandra Adams had grabbed Mel as she was in mid-ignore and hustled her away to a quiet spot beside the school trophy cabinet.

'Mel. You know I missed Ambrosia's party with that virus that's been going round?'

'You struck lucky, Sandra. Believe me. What about it, anyway?'

'Malcom Atwill. Was he there?'

'Yes. He was done up like a Recording Angel. Why?'

Sandra couldn't have caught the boy-fancying bug, surely? If she'd succumbed, Mel would feel like the last sane person in a mad-house.

'Did he get off with anybody?'

Good old Sandra, straight to the point. 'All he got was Ambrosia's welcome embrace, as far as I know. Why?'

'Because I don't trust him. He's weird.' Sandra lowered her voice to a whisper. 'I think he wants me to go out with him.'

'You're right, he is weird!' Mel bit her tongue. 'I didn't mean it that way. Sorry.'

'Don't be,' said Sandra. 'I know I've got the figure of a beached whale. But I've got my pride. And I certainly won't be bought!'

'What?'

'You remember that poetry partner session before half-term?'

'I'll never forget it, Sandra.'

'Well, this is what Malcolm Atwill gave me.' Mel was handed a sheet of paper that had been crumpled, then unfolded.

Come out with me, I'm not being funny
You can charge a fee, I've got the money

'Bad joke, Sandra. He didn't say he was serious, did he?'

'Not in so many words, no. But if it was a joke it wasn't funny. And if it wasn't a joke then it definitely wasn't funny. Either way, I was ready to land one on him.'

The racket that Crumb Carmichael had gone over to sort out during her debate with Robbie Brookes, remembered Mel.

Sandra stuffed the page back in her bag. 'Lucky for him, he apologised. Said it was the first thing that came into his head. But I don't know so much. Since then he's been giving me funny looks.'

'He gives everybody funny looks. They all do, Sandra. It's because their heads are changing shape. Their skulls are getting bigger but their brains aren't keeping up.'

'You don't think there's anything in it, then?'

'His head? Nah. Robbie Brookes thought my poem was about him and it certainly wasn't.'

Sandra laughed. 'I heard about the punch bowl. Good one! I'll be following your example. If that creep Atwill so much as mentions money again, I'll strangle him with my bare hands. I'm not cheap, you know.'

For a moment Mel thought she might be making another joke against herself. But, no. She seemed to be fighting back tears.

'I know you're not, Sandra,' she said. 'I know you're not.'

*

Talk about a smooth operation! thought Robbie. *A surgeon with the slickest scalpel known to medical science couldn't have done it smoother!*

Hayley had looked a bit surprised when he'd wheeled her into Zyg's place rather than the Ritz, but once she'd had the full gushing welcome from Mrs Zyg she'd soon softened up.

A glass of Coke and a few of Mrs Zyg's top delicacies later, and it had been back outside for a quick detour down the handy alleyway which leads round to the back of the shop.

Twilly and Greg had strolled by dead on schedule, started the clock, and bingo – forty-eight seconds later he'd upped his Hayley credits nicely, as his log now showed:

Hayley: 48 x tariff of 21 = 1008
Ambrosia: 20 x tariff of 15 = 300
Total: 1,308

Less than a hundred short of Daz. Hit the maximum with Hayley on Saturday at the school firework display and he'd be in the second place and catching up fast!

*

It was impossible. But it was there in front of him, in her green felt-tip writing.

Thinking it would be a good idea to keep Hayley on the boil, Robbie had arranged to meet her at the Zygs' for a quick can of something. As he could bank on Mrs Zyg to give them at least one on the house, it wouldn't cost him anything – and he'd get some alley-practice into the bargain!

But she'd been late. Ten minutes, fifteen minutes, then twenty, which was when a shaggy-haired first year had stuck his head round the door.

'Oy, mate. Your name Blobby?'

'Robbie.'

'This is for you, then. Crumpet give me five pee to bring it.' And he'd dumped an envelope on the table. Robbie ripped it open.

Dear Robbie,
Sorry, I can't make it. A friend who I was friendly with before I was friendly with you wants to be friendly with me again and not friendly with somebody I thought he was being too friendly with but he wasn't

because she was being friendly with everybody so I've decided to be friends with him again.

Hayley

He couldn't understand the riddle, but the message was clear. He'd been dumped. His face must have shown as much, because Mr Zyg puffed over with a cleaning cloth to boom, 'Robbie. Your face like wet weekend in Warsaw! What happen, the girl kiss you bye-byes?'

'Yeah,' said Robbie ruefully. 'Still. That's life, eh?'

Mr Zyg nodded. 'Is true. Even my Frieda leaves me standing the once.' The punch-line wasn't long in arriving. 'She run off and I not fast enough to catch up!'

He started laughing fit to bust, till it turned into a rasping wheeze and he had to flop down on a chair. As ever, Mrs Zyg was at his side in an instant, waiting for him to recover.

'Robbie's girl-friend not turn up,' Mr Zyg told her between coughs, 'so I telling him about when you not turn up that time.'

'What time?' asked Robbie, unable to imagine the pair of them ever having a row.

'Ah,' said Mrs Zyg. 'He mean the time I hear him saying to his pal, "I meeting my woman at the dance-hall." Hah! I say to myself, you show him, Frieda. You *a* woman, yah, but you not *his* woman, like you a bag of onions or a pair of boots. You a person! He not own you! So I stay at home and wait for him to call. He does, too!'

Satisfied that Mr Zyg was all right again, she bent down and gave him a kiss on the cheek before heading off into the shop to serve a customer who'd just jangled through the door.

Mr Zyg smiled. 'Only that once, it happens,' he said in the softest voice Robbie had ever heard him use. 'I find out from my pal why she got angry and I never give her chance to do it again. I prove I want her and nobody else.'

'How d'you manage that?'

'How you think? I ask her to marry me.'

Robbie grinned. 'So she ended up being your woman after all!'

But, surprising him, Mr Zyg didn't guffaw like he'd expected. He shook his head. 'That where you wrong, Robbie. I ask her because I am knowing then I want to be her man. Very different. Very different indeed.'

*

Who could you trust? Nobody! Robbie had turned up at the firework display and who was Hayley going 'Ooh' and 'Aah' with? Darren puffin' Hogg!

How had her note started? *A friend who I was friendly with before I was friendly with you wants to be friendly with me again...*

So that's the friend she'd been on about. Daz! He must have sought her out, told her about Ambrosia's one-person welcoming party and persuaded her to ditch him. Some puffin' friend! Robbie collared him the moment the last rocket plunged to earth and he saw Hayley trot off to buy a hot dog and a drink.

'You double-crossing sprocket! You talked her into dumping me, didn't you?'

'Yep,' admitted Daz, straight out.

'But I hadn't hit top whack with her,' moaned Robbie. 'I had twelve seconds to go!'

'And I've got forty-six seconds to go, Brookesie,' said Daz, rubbing his hands together. 'Though if that's still the situation when this evening's over I'll be very disappointed!'

'And I thought we were mates,' said Robbie.

'We are, Brookesie, we are. But as they say...all's fair in snog and war!'

The sprocket. The devious, dirty, double-dealing sprocket. If you can't trust your mate, who can you trust?

*

Robbie's dream, a vengeful one in which a certain D. Hogg was sitting astride a bonfire pleading for mercy whlle he toyed with a box of matches, was interrupted by somebody shaking him by the arm. He woke up to find his mum kneeling beside his bed, dressed and ready to go out.

'Robbie,' she said quietly, 'I've decided to go up to Gran's for a few days.'

'Why?' he blinked. 'Is there something wrong?'

His gran had been a bit dodgy on her pins for a while. She'd had a nasty fall a year or so before and they'd all had to shoot up to see her in a hurry, two hundred and fifty miles with the OM moaning every inch of the way about why she couldn't move nearer.

'Wrong?' said Mum. 'Not with Gran, no.'

'Who, then?'

'With...me and your dad...'

Gemma, he thought at once. *If you can't trust your mate, who can you trust?*

Mum didn't give him a chance to ask more, just stood up very quickly.

'I think it'll do us both good to have a couple of days on our own. So I thought I'd give Gran a surprise. You'll be all right? Yes, of course you will. There's plenty of food in the freezer. Dinner money's in the tin in the cupboard. I'll see you in a few days.'

By the time Robbie had thrown on some clothes and followed her downstairs she was half-way along the road, pulling her case behind her like an air hostess heading for a flight.

For the rest of the day he took refuge in *Graveyard III*, stopping only to defrost burgers and heaps of oven-ready chips and going to bed early only to wake up at midnight with gut-ache.

Then he looked out of the window to see it chucking it down with rain and his school trousers still on the line.

Great. Puffin' great.

Ninth Week of Term
Popping the Question

Monday 9th November

Even though I am taking industrial inaction as regards English, I am determined to continue making entries in this log. Not because of any simmering feelings for my teacher, may his stanzas drop off, but as a record of revenge wreaked.

2-3 p.m. Carmichael's convoy

Emotion #1, re: Carmichael: satisfaction, bordering on contentment.

Emotion #2, re: Brookes: unhappiness, bordering on panic. I was much more encouraging to my poetry partner today than I intended to be. Looking back, this must have been because it helped me achieve emotion #1.

(Note: this is a useful lesson. I know now that one emotion can affect another - leaving one with mixed emotions, ha-ha! On second thoughts, it's not funny at all. It's true.)

Carmichael's idea of a poetry tour had come as quite a

surprise. He hadn't taken them to an airy-fairy, tree-strewn, golden-leafed place, as Robbie had expected. No, he'd taken them to the scene of Daz's maxi-triumph with Zoë – the tombstone-strewn churchyard!

Through a metal swing gate, along a path winding its way through the lopsided gravestones, to an open spot beside the flint rear wall of the church. There he stopped and waited for them to gather round before taking out a poetry book.

'Listen carefully, please. This is from a poem by Percy Bysshe Shelley.

'When the lamp is shattered,
    The light in the dust lies dead –
When the cloud is scattered,
    The rainbow's glory is shed...'

He paused, scowled fiercely at a giggling Hayley McLeod in a way that Robbie hadn't seen before, then went on:

'When the lute is broken,
    Sweet tones are remembered not;
When the lips have spoken,
    Loved accents are soon forgot.'

Closing the book, Carmichael stood looking gloomily thoughtful, as if he was still lost in the poem. Finally he asked them, 'What do you think?'

Daz raised his left hand, his right remaining attached to Hayley's waist like a wheel clamp. 'I think it's a very suitable poem for this place, Mr Carmichael,' he said, trying to keep a straight face. 'Dead good, in fact!'

It was the sort of crack that all the lads had made since the start of term and which, Robbie had to hold up his hands and say, Carmichael had regularly turned to his advantage. But not today. Today they seemed to be dealing with a different bloke altogether.

'Detention, Hogg!' snapped the teacher. 'I've just about had enough of the stupid comments I get from this class. Has anybody got anything sensible to say?'

A hushed silence fell across the group, the sort that nobody wants to break. So it was with some surprise that Mel heard the silence broken by the voice of her poetry partner saying something even more surprisingly sensible.

'He's right though, isn't he?' said Robbie.

Defending Daz the Hayley-snatcher had been the last thing on his mind. In fact, if there'd been an empty hole around, Robbie would have gladly shoved him in it. But something about Carmichael's poem had got to him.

'What I mean is,' he heard himself saying, 'it's a poem about things dying.' He waved at the mouldering gravestones all round them. 'Like the people buried here. That's what the poem's saying, isn't it? Things live for a while, then they snuff it. All gone.'

That's what had got to him. *Mum and the OM's marriage is going the same way. Dying. Maybe it's already dead.*

Another voice chipped in. 'How about hopes and dreams?' said Mel Bradshaw, all firm-like. 'How about love and stuff like that? They can die as well, can't they?'

'Yes, Miss Bradshaw. They can. And take it from me, grief is as powerful an emotion as joy.'

It had all got a bit heavy for Robbie. He wasn't feeling great, Mel Bradshaw was looking like she had a bad headache and Carmichael's face was as cheerful as a chimp's rear end.

So it was almost a relief when the teacher said bleakly, 'Look around with your poetry partners for five minutes. Make notes.'

Carmichael hadn't said what to make notes on, but by then it was too late. Daz had already begun to manoeuvre Hayley towards the spot where Zoë Freeman's understanding had bubbled over and the rest of the group were scattering in all directions.

Robbie took a hesitant step towards Mel Bradshaw. *This is going to be as much fun as a visit to the dentist,* he thought, *especially if she's got another fruit salad tucked out of sight.* But, strangely, Mel wasn't looking at him like he was something she'd just scraped off her shoe. She was moving towards him, half-smiling.

'Come on, Robbie,' she said, slipping her arm through his and leading him off in the opposite direction to the rest of the mob. 'Let's look at some epitaphs. Not here, though. There's too many weeds around.'

It had been an emotional reaction, Mel knew that. A sudden, crazy desire to show Carmichael just how much she didn't care for him by snuggling up to Robbie Brookes, class clown.

Except that…only moments before, Robbie Brookes hadn't been clowning at all. He'd shown the first sign ever of being sensitive and sensible. But, she smartly reminded herself, only the first sign. The instant they were out of Carmichael's sight, she let go of his arm.

But even that small touch had been enough to put Robbie in a spin. Talk about a U-turn! *One minute she's showing me all the warmth of a fridge-freezer, the next she's turning almost tropical,* he thought. It seemed like a good chance to set things straight.

'Mel,' he said, 'that…er, y'know…Hallowe'en party. I was out of order.'

'Me too, I suppose. I don't know what came over me.'

'I know what came over me,' replied Robbie. 'And it was wet.'

She actually laughed! Robbie felt like he'd struck gold. So when they got near some headstones and Mel suggested he jot down a few epitaphs just to make it look as if they were doing things properly, it was like a lion-tamer asking her furry friend to jump through a flaming hoop.

Surprisingly, though, she hadn't brought her Carmichael log-book to write in. And, jammed full of incriminating *Snogathon* details as it was, he certainly hadn't brought his!

Robbie's luck was in. His too-small reserve trousers, fished out of the wardrobe in a hurry once he'd given up hope of his best pair drying out after their overnight soaking, had been giving his goolies a tough time all day. He'd cursed them on more than one occasion. But now he blessed them. Scrabbling in the back pocket, he found a sheet of folded-up paper. Discovering an only slightly leaky biro in his jacket pocket, Robbie jotted as Mel read from different tombstones.

'Gone, but not forgotten.'

'Though he walks beside me no more,
his footprints remain.'

'Until we meet again.'

When the five minutes were up he nobly handed the paper over. Stuffing the sheet in her bag, Mel headed off with him bringing up the rear – only to track back and repeat her arm-entwining act as they turned the corner to head in Carmichael's direction.

It was Robbie's big chance. Now or never. It had all come as a big surprise, one he couldn't explain, but for all that here he was and there she was, Micro Mel, not so micro any more, really nice-looking in fact and, as if that wasn't enough, on a *Snogathon* tariff that was positively stratospheric.

So he said, 'Mel. How'd you like to, er…y'know, come out with me?'

He wondered for a moment if she hadn't heard. She didn't say yes. She didn't say no. She didn't say anything, just kept him in suspense until they were near enough standing on Dave Carmichael's toes.

Only then did she say, 'Go out with you, Robbie? I'd love to.'

Puffin hell! Ya-hooooooooooooo!!

*

Tuesday 10th November

8.10 a.m. Emotional condition: feeling sick.

Why, out of 101 other ways of showing Dave Carmichael how little I now think of him - dumb insolence, snide poems, etc., etc. - could I have believed that hearing me agree to go out with Robbie Brookes would be the best?

Medical condition: feeling sick.

I've got that virus lucky Sandra caught, the one that kept her away from the Hallowe'en party.

9.38 a.m. At home, and staying here. Above conditions still apply.

1.55 p.m. Feeling worse. Can hardly move, except to roll over and puke my mother's 'this will make you feel better' potions into the bowl at my side.

10.20 p.m. Decision made. Assuming I live, I'll make up some excuse to give Robbie Brookes: I'm not allowed out with a boy till I've completed my schooling, painted the skirting boards, converted the loft - anything.

The other lads couldn't have been greener if they'd been little green men who'd landed in Greenland.

'Micro!' gasped Greg. 'You're going out with Micro?'

'Not so much of the Micro, giblet,' said Robbie, loving every minute. 'That's my babe you're talking about.'

'And she's not so microscopic any more,' growled Daz, 'as we're all agreed. Chesty will be looking over her shoulder soon, I reckon.'

'That's a physical impossibility,' said Twilly.

'How's the Chesty epic going, Daz?' asked Robbie.

'Filled your log-book yet? Or has Hayley been taking up too much of your writing time?'

'Making progress,' leered Daz, before making to wring Robbie's neck as he remembered the main topic of conversation. 'Micro Mel! You giblet! I mean, she's on a tariff of...'

Robbie winked. Daz had got there at last. They all had. But, as usual, it was Twilly who put it into numbers.

'Ninety,' he said, like he was a judge passing the death sentence. 'Lads, this could be the winning move.'

*

It was an emotional problem, all right. Worth committing to paper to see if that helped. Robbie turned to a fresh page in his Carmichael log-book.

Fact: a maxi-score with Mel will be worth
60 x 90 = 5,400 credits!

Achieving that on any occasion between now and the end of term would put him so far out in front that the *Snogathon* loot would be as good as his!

Problem: So, do I make a bid first time out?

Mel was a prickly one. Pricklier than a bramble that's

been to the bramble-sharpener. The last thing he wanted to do was make a move too soon, get her annoyed and miss out altogether. On the other hand, as every football manager knew, it was better to have points in the bag than games in hand.

Question: Where to take her?

What he needed was an outing that gave him a chance to try it on without making it seem like he was trying it on.

Answer: Take her to a place where touching, grabbing, squeezing and every other -ing comes naturally.

Next question: Where the puffin' hell can that be?

*

To quote Robbie Brookes in the churchyard: 'Things live for a while, then they snuff it. All gone.' It was true, Mel had to admit. Everything dies in the end. Even stomach bugs. (Well, either they did or you did.) It had been on Thursday that subtle signs she was on the mend had shown themselves. Like, she'd started to argue with her mother again.

'Stay at home tomorrow as well,' Mrs Bradshaw had

insisted in the face of Mel's protests, 'just to make sure.'

Whatever that means, thought Mel the next morning. Feeling more alive by the minute meant she was now starting to die of boredom. It was going to be a toss-up between watching daytime TV or doing some homework. No contest. It would have to be the homework.

She began emptying her school bag, the first time she'd touched it since Monday's poetry parade with Carmichael. *Probably where I got the germ*, she thought. Out came Science books, Geography books, French books. Finally, cowering beneath the lot, she found a folded-up scribbled-on sheet of paper.

Mel glanced at the scribbles. *Gone, but not forgotten. Though he walks beside me no more, his footprints remain. Until we meet again.* The reminder of the mad agreement she'd made and the need to put Robbie Brookes off next Monday – with a crowbar if that's what it took – made her wince.

She grabbed one edge of the paper in each hand, and was about to rip it into satisfyingly small pieces when she noticed that Brookes's scrawl wasn't the only writing it carried. There was something printed on its reverse.

In the form of a scroll, it was...

*

Friday 13th November

10.13 a.m.

Emotion: blind, unadulterated fury.

Words and phrases that have sprung to mind: agony, torment, suffering, anguish, woe, misery, distress, cry-for-mercy, put-me-out-of-my-misery.

1.10 p.m.

Emotion: blind fury has mellowed. It's now open-eyed, cold-hearted, beat-him-to-a-pulp fury.

Words: as above, plus: scum, trash, dreg.

4.14 pm.

Emotion: desire for revenge.

Mel threw aside her log-book and picked up her mobile. She scanned the name list, punched in during her initial wave of got-me-own-mobile enthusiasm whether she thought she'd ever call the person or not. She found the name she was after. The name of the one person she could think of who'd feel the same way as her...

*

Cracked it! thought Robbie. *There must be something about a Saturday. Frees the brain up to get on with some non-school stuff.* Whatever the explanation was, he had definitely, undoubtedly cracked it. It was a moment worth logging:

Touching?

Grabbing?

Squeezing?

Solution: Obvious. Take Mel Bradshaw ice skating!

He could see it all. She'd slip over, he'd help her up. She'd slip over again, he'd help her up again – holding on a bit longer this time. After an hour of that, clinging to him all leaf-like would feel like second nature!

And there was that short cut from the main road to the skating rink, the little lane where cars were always breaking down late at night suffering from steamed-up window problems. Plenty of observation spots down there!

It was perfect. What a pity he'd have to wait until Monday to suggest it. Of course, he could always try ringing her...

No, maybe not. He didn't want to be overheard. Besides, every time he'd gone near the phone lately he'd been subjected to I'm-gonna-want-to-try-her-again-in-a-minute looks from the OM.

His mum was still at his gran's. She'd called Robbie regularly to check that he wasn't starving, usually before the OM was due home from work. More than once Robbie had asked her when she was coming back.

'Not yet, Robbie. I'm not ready yet.'

He suspected she was saying the same thing to the OM whenever he called her, though in rather different words. It sounded like it, judging from the OM's end of the conversation coming through the ceiling like bullets.

'Look, it's over! It meant nothing and now it's over! I won't see Gemma again. I've told her. Can't you understand that? It's over!'

'Is Mum coming home soon?' Robbie had asked after one session.

'She'd better be,' he'd growled. 'Or I'll go up there and drag her back by the hair.'

The OM called it the no-nonsense approach. What didn't seem to be sinking in to him was that it wasn't working. But Robbie didn't think he knew any other way.

He decided to leave calling Mel for a little while. For all the OM's desire to have another go at insisting Mum come home, he wouldn't forsake his Sunday lunchtime drinking session. Robbie would have time on his own then.

In the meantime he would dream of the *Snogathon* points coming his way when he got his skates on with Micro Mel!

*

Carmichael might have to struggle with me, thought Robbie next morning, *but he'd more than have his work cut out teaching the Zygs something about emotion.*

As he collected his pay, he told them he probably couldn't come in and help out after school that coming Wednesday.

'You have the date, yah?' boomed Mr Zyg. 'You take my tip and tell that girl she's the only one for you?'

'No,' said Robbie. 'Different girl.'

Mr Zyg laughed. 'Hah! You look around first? Good! I do that too!'

'Oh, you did, did you?' said Mrs Zyg, hands on hips.

'Of course!' said Mr Zyg, then reached out to cup her face in his hands. 'But only till I meet you. Then I know it waste of time looking more. I not find better!'

That's what Robbie had had in mind. There only seemed to be one emotion the Zygs knew anything about: lovey-dovey slop-slop. No arguments. No grief. No OM-versus-Mum slanging matches.

Lucky beggars.

Mel handed Sandra Adams the sheet of paper. Perched on the end of Mel's bed, Sandra proceeded to read the rules aloud, one quivering hand holding the paper while her other clutched a ball of Mel's duvet in an ever-tightening grip of steel. Mel listened in silence, even though she'd read them so often she'd be able to take them as her specialist subject if they ever brought back *Mastermind* on TV.

'"All participants in the *Snogathon* will be sworn to absolute secrecy..."' growled Sandra. '"The winner of the *Snogathon* will be the contestant scoring the most credits by the end of the term...Credits will be scored by making progress in a snogful encounter..."' She looked at Mel. 'Does that mean what I think it means?'

'That they've got some smutty competition going? That's how I read it.' Mel drew Sandra's attention to the numbers at the bottom of the sheet. 'And by the look of it, some of us are more valuable than others.'

'Atwill,' breathed Sandra, looking as if sheets of flame were about to shoot out of her nostrils. 'He *was* serious. Look! Land his greasy gob on me for any length of time and he'd run up a score like a lottery winner's cheque.'

Mel tried to soften the insult. 'Same goes for me, Sandra. I'm up there with the high scores as well.'

Sandra shook her head. 'But not because you look like an all-in wrestler and only a calculating weasel like Malcolm Atwill would want to try it on with you. They've given you a high score because they think you're a toughie, Mel.'

'You reckon?'

'After the way you socked Darren Hogg that time? I'm amazed Robbie Brookes had the bottle to ask you out...'

She stopped. Mel knew why. Obviously the tale was all round school. 'Do not mention Robbie Brookes,' she said. 'I had my reasons. But now…'

Sandra was looking expectantly at her, eyes glittering. 'Now we pay them back, right? Teach them they can't treat us like…like…snog objects!'

Mel couldn't help laughing. 'A snog object? What's that?'

Even Sandra giggled. 'Like a sex object. Beginner's version.'

Her tone changed as she snatched up the *Snogathon* rules again, glaring at them as if they were the lines of a wicked spell. 'These are dis-gusting! Look at Rule Five! "'Credits will only be credited after the details of the snogful encounter have been verified by two witnesses."' She looked aghast as the full meaning sank in. 'Witnesses? So if I had…did…with Malcolm Atwill… then two of the others would be…?'

'Watching? That's how I read it, Sandra.'

Which means Hayley must have been watched more often than an old TV movie!

'But…can't we *do* something?' cried Sandra.

'Like what?'

'Blackmail. Get that squirt Atwill in a corner, show him these rules and say we're going to shop him if he doesn't hand over his credit card and pin number.'

'You're not serious?'

'Why not? Have you got a better idea?'

'Show them to the other girls. We could all band together and demand action.' *Not that I know what action*, thought Mel.

To say Sandra wasn't convinced was putting it mildly. 'Band together? With us? Come on, Mel. They've near enough been throwing themselves at the boys all term. Hayley's launched herself more often than a space shuttle.'

'So,' sighed Mel, 'what's left?'

'We take direct action!'

'You don't mean you really do want to blackmail Malcolm Atwill?'

'Unless I can have my first choice, which would be to carry him to a sound-proofed room where you'd sit on him while I whipped his trousers down and got to work with a pair of garlic crushers.'

'I think I'd prefer his credit card and pin number!'

'Melanie,' purred Sandra, 'by the time I was finished with my garlic crushers, everything he owns would be ours. He'd have nothing left. And I mean *nothing*!'

Although she was joking – at least, Mel thought she was joking – her spirit of revenge was starting to become infectious.

'Why stop at Malcolm Atwill,' she said. 'All four of

them must be in it. We could pick them off one by one.'

'Just what I was planning to do with my garlic crushers!'

'Sandra, please! Besides...there might be another way...'

'It's got to be painful. I insist.'

'It is. But it's a different kind of pain. One boys hate. It's called humiliation. Show them up. Laugh at them.'

Sandra, Amazon Adams, the target of more taunts per term than the rest of the school put together, thought about it for a moment. 'You're right, Mel. Being laughed at is painful.'

'I don't know if it compares with the garlic crushers.'

'It does, take it from me. Humiliation crushes your soul.'

It wasn't an easy statement to follow. Which meant that, all in all, it was very convenient for the silence to be interrupted by the ringing of the phone...

Robbie checked his watch, snatched up his log and began writing. Footballers recorded the key moments on the road to their cup-winning triumphs, didn't they? Well, the phonecall he'd just ended was definitely going to be a key moment on the road to his *Snogathon*-winning triumph!

Sunday 1.50 p.m. Rang Mel. Suggested ice-skating this Wednesday, 6 to 7 p.m. She said great, love to, what a fantastic idea even though I'm not very good at it and will need guiding round a lot, meet you there because that's easiest for me.

You want an emotion, Mr Carmichael? How about – *yeaaaaahhh!*

Anticipated emotion on Wednesday: *lovey-dovey slop-slop!!*

Roll on Wednesday!

Although, thought Robbie, with a bit of luck he could get in some preliminary softening-up activity before then. If Carmichael was helpful tomorrow, maybe there'd be a cosy poetry partner session in which he could snuggle up to Mel and talk about whatever they were supposed to talk about.

Epitaphs, wasn't it?

Now where had he put them?

Tenth Week of Term
Losing the Plot

Puffin' hell! Puffin' puffin' hell!!!

Robbie hadn't slept. He'd only worked it out slowly, but once he had it had been enough to turn him into a nervous wreck.

The epitaphs...he'd written them on a folded-up sheet of paper.

No folded-up sheets of paper in his bag, though.

Try his jacket pockets. No. Trouser pockets? No.

Hang on, Monday had been too-tight reserve trousers day. When he'd taken them off after eight hours of discomfort his thing had looked like a concertina. Maybe he'd left them there. He'd reached to the back of his wardrobe and tried the pockets of his reserve trousers. No folded-up sheet of paper.

Then he'd remembered: him nobly handing it over and Mel Bradshaw stuffing it in her bag. That's why he couldn't find it. He'd given it to Mel.

Well done, Brookesie. Brownie-points scored, there. Lucky you had that sheet of paper handy!

Funny that. Why had it been there? Sheets of paper weren't the sort of thing he usually stored in his pockets. Especially his reserve trousers, which he only wore when circumstances absolutely forced him to. Like his usual ones being left on the line in a monsoon, or put in the wash after getting muddy playing football so that he had to sit through a *Snogathon* rules meeting shifting about on a library bench seat like he'd got some kind of twitching lurgy.

Snogathon rules meeting...

The rules sheet and opening tariffs...

Another memory. The vote. The others looking at him. He gives them a knowing smile. He nonchalantly folds his rules sheet. He casually slides it into his back trouser pocket.

His back reserve trousers pocket!

Puffin' hell! Puffin' puffin' hell!!! He'd accidentally given Melanie Bradshaw the *Snogathon* rules sheet!

And so it was that Robbie had spent all morning avoiding any eye contact with Mel Bradshaw. That had been bad enough. But sitting through Carmichael's lesson wondering if they were going to be sent off to a poetry partner session any minute was like being in a condemned cell.

Fortunately, Carmichael had spent most of the hour talking about the poet Shelley's private life. In spite of his guts feeling like they were made of lead piping, Robbie couldn't help but be interested in the sordid tales of how Shelley managed to talk not one, but two sixteen-year-old girls into running off with him! But then, with no more than five minutes to go, the teacher called a halt.

'In the time left, can you get together with your poetry partners, please. Talk about the poem I read to you in the churchyard last week. And compare it with whatever you noticed when you looked round...'

Robbie's legs started quivering. He didn't want to move. But apparently Mel did. She was heading his way. He braced himself for a right-hander, or worse. It didn't come.

'Hello, Robbie,' smiled Mel, instead. 'Have you got the epitaphs?'

She's asking me if I've got them? Robbie's poor brain couldn't cope. 'M-me? No. Maybe. Er...'

Had he got it all wrong? Maybe he hadn't given them to her. Maybe he'd just lost them.

The first part of Mel's plan swung smoothly into action. Burying her head in her bag she innocently pulled out the sheet – the sheet she'd carefully folded back the way it had been.

'Yes! That's them!' squeaked Robbie.

Mel sighed. 'I haven't had time to look at them, Robbie. What with being ill and all that...'

She'd got them – but she hadn't looked at them! He

was safe! Safe, safe, safe!

Waves of relief sweeping over him, Robbie whipped the sheet back as calmly as he could.

'No problem!' he cried. 'You probably couldn't have read my writing anyway. Tell you what, I'll write them out again. Y'know, neat like. Then we could talk about them.'

'Are you sure?'

'Sure I'm sure. Never been surer!'

Mel gave him a smile. 'Well, if you like, Robbie. Maybe we could talk about them on Wednesday?'

Wednesday! She was thinking about Wednesday! The crisis really was over! He could get back to concentrating on the future, the delightful future...

'Right. Good idea. I'm really looking forward to Wednesday, Mel. Are you?'

'I can't say how much, Robbie.'

'It's going to be cool.'

'Skating rinks usually are, Robbie.'

*

Wednesday 17th November.

4.05 p.m.

Emotion: nervous anticipation!

Knowing that Robbie Brookes doesn't know that we know about their Snogathon is delicious. Since Monday he's checked we're meeting outside the ice rink, checked the time, checked just about everything except my physical fitness. He was probably hoping to do that after the skating!

No chance! Sandra and I have it all sorted. We were born in the wrong era. Napoleon could have done with us planning his battles if the job we've done on our après-skate tactics is anything to go by. They're like a military operation. I'm going to write them out one more time to fix them in my mind:

'S' hour (i.e. 6 p.m.): Skating session begins

'S+10': Girl-gathering at Sandra's house, supposedly for CD-playing and general chatting. But instead she tells them what's been going on, submits the copy we made of the Snogathon sheet as evidence, then whips them up into an outraged mob.

'S+45': Sandra supervises making of water and flour bombs.

'S+55': Vigilante squad leave Sandra's house and head for the ice rink.

'S+59': Squad in position.

'S+60': Skating session ends.

'S+61': I refuse any offers of hand-holding in coffee bar, etc., etc., and guide Robbie Brookes into the trap.

'S+62': Humiliation begins!

Wednesday. 8.20 p.m.

Just got home and feel like writing something. Don't know why. Make me feel better after the terrible time I've just been through, maybe? Because that's what it was. A terrible, puffin' disaster. And if I feel bad, how does she feel?

Robbie paused, closed his eyes, sighed. It was no good. Too tough a job. He made a final note.

Carmichael, I know you gave us these books to log our emotions in. OK, and I know I've messed about. But now, when I really want to do the job properly, when I really feel as if sitting down and pouring it all out will help, I can't find the right words. I'm not sure I ever will...

*

He'd been ready for his skating date an hour early. He'd got changed. He'd run the OM's electric shaver over his top lip. He'd sprayed under his arms. He'd brushed his teeth with minty-taste toothpaste for extra shine and stay-fresh breath. He was all ready.

Now he was desperate to kill an hour. How

desperate? Desperate enough to look at the homework Carmichael had fired at them via Chesty Westy just before home time, that's how desperate! 'Find another poem about life and death, then write one of your own.'

Useless. How could he think about dead bodies when the prospect of grappling with Mel Bradshaw's real, live, not-so-microscopic one was on the horizon? He couldn't. He felt like a gum-chewing footballer before a big match, pacing up and down the dressing room when all he wants is to get on with the action.

Chewing gum, thought Robbie. *That's a point.* The minty-taste toothpaste could wear off and give way to the onion-stuffed burgers he'd eaten for lunch. Chewing gum, that's what he needed. The Zygs' shop was on the way. He'd get some there. It would help pass the time.

Chewing gum: long-lasting, fresh, kiss-me-taste-it-and-come-back-for-another-one chewing gum, that's what Robbie was still thinking about when he jangled through the Zygs' door.

There was nobody around. Now that was odd, because they were usually both there, snuggling up in that way they had. And even when Mrs Zyg had nipped out to drive an order round to some home-bound customer, as Robbie had often seen her do during his after-school shelf-stacking sessions, it had been to leave Mr Zyg perched on his stool by the till.

'Anybody home?' Robbie yelled. 'Kid in need of service round here!'

No answer.

He drifted into the café part. The coffee percolator was gurgling to itself, as if it had just come to the boil. The door behind the counter was ajar. Perhaps Mr Zyg had taken the chance to try to lug in some cans from the storeroom while it was quiet. It was a job Mrs Zyg had asked Robbie to do before now, always when Mr Zyg wasn't listening.

'It not good for him, carrying heavy things. But he not listen. Sometimes I think I marry a deaf man!'

Robbie lifted the counter flap, went round, looked through the door.

Mr Zyg was on the floor.

In a funny way he looked fine, just like he was having a snooze, except that Robbie knew he wasn't. Mr Zyg was lying at a funny angle. His mouth was half-open and a dribble of saliva was trickling out. Beside him was the big box it looked like he'd been trying to move.

He ran out of the storeroom, shouting for Mrs Zyg at the top of his voice even though he knew in his heart she wasn't there. If she was, she'd have been within touching distance of her husband, as always.

Then he rang 999. The ambulance was quick: a couple of minutes, five at the most. Mrs Zyg still hadn't returned. Robbie told them what he could while they lifted Mr Zyg onto a stretcher, covered him with a red blanket, then trundled him out to the ambulance's open doors.

'Will he be all right?' Robbie asked. 'His wife will be back soon.'

'He's still breathing. But we can't wait. Can anybody hang on and tell her what's happened?'

There was a little clutch of spectators watching, as if it was a real, live television programme. Robbie didn't see anybody he knew. They'd all heard what was said, but nobody had offered. What choice did he have?

'I will,' Robbie heard himself say. 'She's not long usually.' The ambulance wailed off. He locked the shop door and waited.

Mrs Zyg was the best part of forty minutes coming, delayed for a gossip by the old dear she was delivering to, then by discovering she'd run over a nail on the way and got a flat tyre. Robbie threw open the door to meet her.

'What is wrong?' she said at once. 'Where is my Zygmunt?'

Robbie explained as fast as he could, waiting with every word for Mrs Zyg to have hysterics. But she didn't. She just gave a long, tearless kind of sigh as if it was something she'd been expecting for a while.

She asked him to go to the hospital with her, act as navigator round the back streets. On the way she asked Robbie to tell her again where he'd found Mr Zyg, what he'd looked like, every little detail.

'It sounds like the stroke,' she said softly. 'It come again.'

'Stroke?'

'Bleeding in the brain. Zygmunt have a small one eight years ago. He laid up for a while, but get over it. Mostly.'

'Except for his leg?' Mr Zyg's limp.

'Yah. End of dancing.'

Mrs Zyg parked the car in the first spot she found. Robbie hurried with her to the A & E entrance. Questions, answers, directions. Soon they were upstairs on sticky seats opposite a sign reading: 'Intensive Care Unit'. Eventually a woman in a white coat came out and confirmed Mrs Zyg's suspicions.

Her husband had had a stroke, possibly a big one. Extent of damage uncertain. He wasn't in any immediate danger. Mrs Zyg could see him in a while. Would she wait?

'I wait. We married a long time. If I was going to leave him I do it by now.'

Good one, Mrs Zyg! thought Robbie. *What a dozy puffin' question. Of course she'll wait. Any fool could see that. She'll wait for ever.*

It just seemed natural to ask, 'How long have you been married, Mrs Zyg?'

'Thirty-one years, fifth of December. We meet at a dance.'

'Right. You said. The dancer of your youth.'

'Yah. He different, you know that?'

'You said that as well. Slim, wasn't it?'

'Ah, I make that up a bit! My Zygmunt, he never *that* slim. He never win no Mr Handsome competition, either.'

She smiled at her memories. 'I have enough of that sort come to me, Robbie. "Frieda," they say, "you beautiful girl, I rippling muscle man. We be good together. Why you stick with blobby walnut face, eh? What you see in him?"' She turned suddenly. 'You ever wonder that, Robbie?'

The question had come as such a surprise that Robbie didn't know what to say. He didn't even have time to dream up a lie. He found himself shrugging in a way he knew said, 'Who wouldn't wonder?'

Mrs Zyg placed a hand on his arm. 'Not worry, all do.

"She smasher, he ugly-mug," they think. "How she end up with him?" You want to know?'

How could he say no? It was obviously doing Mrs Zyg good to talk about her husband and, besides, it was a question he'd asked himself enough times. In the films and the magazines it was always the good-looking blokes who ended up with the good-looking girls. How had a pug-ugly like Mr Zyg landed a belter like her?

'Sure,' he said. Bad move.

'Why you think?' Mrs Zyg fired back. She'd caught him on the hop again.

This is becoming worse than one of Carmichael's observation exercises!

Then he'd realised – it was really just the same. What Mrs Zyg was asking him to do was look at Mr Zyg through her eyes instead of his own.

'Because he's...a laugh. He says deadly things to you – but he does it with a smile, so you know he doesn't mean it.'

Unlike the OM and Mum when they're having a go at each other.

'That just one thing,' nodded Mrs Zyg. 'There plenty of others, but they all add up to same. Zygmunt not like the others. Zygmunt treat me like a person, not a beauty body.'

'Except the time he called you his woman!'

Mrs Zyg giggled like she was a girl again. 'Yah! But that day he proved he the man for me.'

'He told me. He asked you to marry him.'

'No, no, that come later. But I know from that day. Because that day he say to me, "Sorry, Frieda." All the toughie-nut looks not mean a thing, Robbie. Man who can say that, he is the real strong man.'

She talked on for a while more, until the white coat came out again and said Mr Zyg seemed to be stable and she could go in and sit with him for a while.

Robbie waited until she came out. There wasn't much point doing anything else. He should have been at the ice rink over two hours ago.

He closed his log-book. *Say sorry?* He could try it. He went down into the hall and dialled Mel's number.

'Er...hi. It's Robbie...' was all he managed before she hung up on him.

Mel slammed the phone down.

Sorry? She was the one who was sorry! Why was it that the only thing you could rely on from the male species was that they'd let you down? First it had been Dave Carmichael turning out to be a fraud. Now it was Robbie Brookes.

Her blood still ran colder than that ice rink when she

thought about the near miss their plan had had. If, after hanging around like a lemon for half an hour, she hadn't called Sandra to stop her sending her part of the plan swinging into action, they'd have all roared up, armed to the teeth, only to discover that the place was a Brookes-free-zone.

Fortunately, Sandra hadn't had time to say anything at all, the girls' conversation having been dominated by Zoë and Ambrosia's critical survey of pop star's bums. But that wasn't the point. *How dare Brookes not turn up to be humiliated!*

Mel had a hard enough time of it the next day as it was, insisting to the others that it was no big deal, she hadn't been stood up really, it wasn't a proper date, she'd only agreed to give him a skating lesson, etc., etc.

'Oh, yes, we believe that – not!'

'You sure it was skating lessons, Mel?'

She'd have told them the whole story just to shut them up if Sandra hadn't put Zoë in a neck-lock, saying that if she didn't wrap up she'd give Zoë's ear an extra piercing, namely with the point of her compass.

Sandra had then taken Mel aside and insisted they could still do what they'd planned.

'Only if it's the garlic-crushing option, Sandra,' glowered Mel. 'I insist. Robbie Brookes deserves nothing less.'

'It's not. And it's not him. Forget him.'

Hadn't Mel said much the same thing to Hayley, when she'd had Greg Morris on the brain? If Hayley could do it, she certainly could.

'Forget him?' said Mel. 'I'll need time, Sandra.' She paused for a nanosecond. 'That's long enough. Who are you thinking of, then?...'

*

So much for saying sorry, thought Robbie next day. Mel Bradshaw wasn't talking to him. She wasn't even looking at him.

Greg and Daz weren't best pleased with him not turning up at the ice rink either – but how could he have been expected to know that lane was overlooked by an eagle-eyed Neighbourhood Watcher? It wasn't his fault that one minute they'd been lounging around, wondering where he'd got to, and the next a squad car had screeched up. Nor that they were given a ten-minute grilling before being sent on their way.

Robbie explained what had happened to Mr Zyg.

Daz tried to make a joke of it. 'What, the big bloke? Who'd they have carrying the stretcher? Superman?'

'Shut up. It wasn't funny.'

'No. Right,' said Daz, only slightly subdued.

Greg couldn't hide his chirpiness, either. 'Looks like you've been and blown it with Micro though,

Brookesie,' he said. 'I reckon the race is between me and Daz now...'

Greg is up to 38 seconds with Purity Meek. Daz is up to 55 with Hayley.

And me? I've just had it up to here, as they say. Meaning, I don't really care. Is that an emotion?

I know what is. The way my guts ache for Mr and Mrs Zyg. Being apart must be torture for them. They're made to be together. I wish they were my parents.

*

By Sunday, Mrs Zyg was open for business again. After a couple of days shut, she'd rung Robbie to make sure he'd be there for his papers as usual.

'How's Mr Zyg?' he'd asked.

He'd called her a couple of times since it happened. The first time she'd said he was sleeping a lot. Next bulletin, he was awake a bit more, and showing he knew what was going on. This time she'd answered, 'Fine, Robbie. They say he doing fine, considering.'

So when he bowled into the shop to be given a big smile, Robbie assumed it was all good news.

'What's the latest, then? Letting him out soon, are they?'

Mrs Zyg shook her head. 'Month. Maybe more. They

have to fix things for here. He need wheelchair, downstairs loo, all sorts.'

'A wheelchair? What, just for a while you mean?'

'No, Robbie. They say probably all time.'

He couldn't understand it. 'But you said he was doing fine, Mrs Zyg…'

'Fine considering he have big stroke, Robbie. But he not able to move all down one side. And he not able to talk. Not yet.'

He couldn't help it. What he was thinking just slipped out. 'And you call that fine?' he shouted. 'Do you? After everything you said you felt about him…'

'Hey! Hey! That enough!'

It was shouted in a tone that could have stopped a runaway rhino in its tracks. 'Sorry,' mumbled Robbie. 'I thought…well, you sounded so cheerful I thought you'd have some good news…'

'Robbie, you not understand? Zygmunt still with me. That *is* good news. If he stop breathing, stuck in coffin – that *bad* news. And they say he can get better. Not great, but better.'

'But – stuck in a wheelchair? And all the rest…'

He was still struggling with the fact that this prospect didn't seem to worry her when she suddenly changed tack completely.

'Hey. You do poetry at your school, yah?'

'When I listen,' grinned Robbie. 'Yeah, we do it. Wordsworth, Shelley. That lot.'

'Me and Zygmunt too. We read. When we first come to this country. Help us learn the English.' She caught the look Robbie gave her and giggled. 'Okey-dokey, so it not work so good. But still we like the poems. So – you know little one by Shelley, starts "Music, when soft voices die," something like that?'

'Not me. But I know a bloke who probably does.'

'Good. You ask him. It not long poem, so not hurt head. It explain why I am saying to myself: "Frieda, the world she keeps turning. People still want to have their newspapers, read their sports stories, eye their Page Three bongos. You open the shop. That what your Zygmunt expect."'

She thrust a huge pile of marked-up papers towards him. 'And he expect you to deliver them!' She laughed. It was nothing near Mr Zyg's decibel level, of course, but Robbie got the message.

'I'm on the way. Say hello to him from me.'

'Yah, I do that. And, hey. There something else I sure he want me to tell you.'

'What's that?'

'Christmas Special *Starkers!* in bag for eighty-nine Bulawayo Avenue!'

Eleventh Week of Term
Wondering Why

The atmosphere hadn't been so much frosty, thought Robbie, as icy. Icier than an icicle in the Ice Age.

After Carmichael had given the command, he and Mel had carried their chairs silently to the same spot in the hall as before. He'd sat down. She'd sat down with her back to him. He'd moved his chair round to her side. She'd folded her arms and stared at the ceiling. He'd tried, for want of a better term, to break the ice.

'Can I tell you why I didn't turn up?'

'No.'

'I had a good reason.'

'No.'

'Will it help if I say I'm sorry?'

'No.'

'Any questions?'

Mel had got into such a good rhythm that she didn't immediately realise that this question hadn't been asked by Robbie Brookes, but by Dave Carmichael as he pulled up a chair to join them.

'No,' she said automatically.

'Yes,' said Robbie.

He'd never thought he'd be so pleased to see a teacher. Or so relieved. Mel's attempt on the nos-per-minute world record had been starting to get monotonous.

'Somebody told me Shelley wrote another poem,' he said.

'I do believe he wrote lots of them, Robbie,' purred Mel. 'Isn't that right, Mr Carmichael? Poets usually buy enough paper for at least a couple of efforts, don't they?'

'Usually, Miss Bradshaw,' said Carmichael without much interest, almost as if he'd put himself in neutral. 'Thinking of one in particular were you, Mr Brookes?'

'One with a first line about music and soft voices.'

'"Music, when soft voices die",' he said at once. 'Why?'

'A lady I know likes it. It's a good one, she says. Reckons I should read it.' Robbie gave him the full message. 'She says it's only short.'

Carmichael flicked an eyebrow, as if giving a gold star to Mrs Zyg, then walked over to some books he'd brought in with him and left sitting on the hall's resident piano. Back he came, flipping the pages. When he'd found what he was looking for he turned the book Robbie's way.

'Eight lines,' he said. 'Short enough?' And with that

he handed the book to Mel and asked, 'Would you care to read it for us, please, Miss Bradshaw?'

Mel was taken aback. Having Robbie Brookes asking about a poem had been disconcerting enough. It was like hearing Zoë Freeman's mum say she'd run out of boy-friends – you just don't expect it. But being asked by a teacher she couldn't stand any more to read a poem to a boy she'd always thought was a total clown was even worse.

Reluctantly, irritably, she began to read.

> 'Music, when soft voices die,
> Vibrates in the memory –
> Odours, when sweet violets sicken,
> Live within the sense they quicken.
>
> Rose leaves, when the rose is dead,
> Are heaped for the beloved's bed;
> And so thy thoughts, when thou are gone,
> Love itself shall slumber on.'

It had been one of the loveliest poems she'd ever read in her whole life. And Robbie Brookes had heard of it? How could anybody be so infuriating!

'So...Shelley's saying there that things live on after they've died, right?' asked Robbie.

Carmichael nodded. If Robbie had been into adverbs, he might have said that he'd nodded thoughtfully. Or reflectively. Or any other adverb that suggested the teacher had more than one thing on his mind.

'Same as those epitaphs I wrote down,' said Robbie, eyeing Mel.

She shrugged.

'*Gone but not forgotten*,' he reminded her. 'That kind of thing. They all say the same: life goes on, but in a different way.'

He turned back to Carmichael. 'It doesn't just flake out, like Shelley said in that bit you read at the churchyard.'

"When the lamp is shattered, the light in the dust lies dead…" recited the teacher, as reflectively as before.

Robbie was struggling to get a grip on something. Something he was surprised to discover felt more important than he'd have believed possible.

'So how can he say both?' he asked. 'How can the same guy write two different things?'

Carmichael went quiet. The question seemed to have put him in some kind of stir. Finally he came up with his answer.

'Because he was like the rest of us, I suppose, Mr Brookes. Human. At times we're depressed. We think everything looks totally bleak. That's the emotion Shelley is expressing when he talks about the lamp. At other times we're hopeful. That's the emotion reflected in the poem Melanie just read.'

He smiled – just about the first time, Robbie realised, that he'd seen him crack his face since they came back after half-term.

'Understand?' said Carmichael.

'Yeah, thanks,' said Robbie.

No wonder it's Mrs Zyg's favourite. She'll take the music vibrating and the love slumbering every time.

*

The person Sandra had suggested was ripe for the humiliation treatment Robbie Brookes had escaped was Darren Hogg.

'We can't do it on our own, though,' she'd said. 'Hayley will have to be told what's been going on.'

The chance to do just that came next day, in the girls' loos. Seeing Hayley go in, Mel and Sandra followed like a pair of determined shadows. Hayley was in front of the mirror.

'Hello, you two,' she trilled. 'Have you decided what you're wearing at the Christmas disco yet?

For a moment, Mel forgot what they'd come in for. 'There's almost four weeks to go, Hay!' she said.

'Tell that to the shops, Melanie! They've had tinsel on sale since May. If I don't get a move on soon I won't get the sort of dress I want. I'm after one that will make my boobs look 34B instead of 32A.'

'You don't need a dress, Hayley,' growled Sandra. 'You need a miracle. Now, pay attention. This is serious. Show her, Mel.'

With the discussion back on track, Mel pulled out the copy of the *Snogathon* rules and tariffs she'd made before returning the original to the laughably panic-stricken Robbie Brookes.

'The boys are having a snogging competition,' said Mel, handing it over. 'To see who can score the most points. That's what Robbie Brookes had in mind with me, till he chickened out.'

'He didn't chicken out,' said Hayley. 'Daz told me. A bloke collapsed at the paper shop where he works. He helped him.'

Mel brushed it aside. Brookes and his excuses weren't on the agenda for this particular meeting. 'A competition, Hay,' she repeated, hoping to lodge the word between her friend's ears.

'A *Snogathon*,' said Sandra. 'Like a *Readathon*, but with girls instead of library books. And so far you've been the most borrowed item,' she added bluntly.

Hayley looked blank. 'What are you saying? That – that Daz...'

'And Robbie Brookes before him, and Greg Morris before him...'

'Have been scoring points for scoring with you,' said Sandra. She jabbed a finger at Rule Five. 'With every one of them in front of a couple of spectators.'

'No. I don't believe it.'

Sandra sighed, clearly considered lifting Hayley by the hair and shaking her till she saw sense, then sighed again. 'Hayley, how do we convince you they're playing a game of pass-the-parcel? And you're the parcel.'

'You can't!' squawked Hayley, slapping the *Snogathon* sheet back at Mel and stomping towards the door. 'Only Daz can do that. And I'm going to ask him, right now!'

'Well, that didn't work out the way we planned,' said Mel as Hayley's footsteps echoed away down the corridor. 'They'll all know now.'

'And my poetry partner sacrifice will have been in vain,' murmured Sandra.

'Your what?'

'Sacrifice. Yesterday, during English. I shoved Malcolm Atwill's poem under his nose...'

'Not – "you can charge a fee, I've got the money"?'

Sandra nodded. 'And I asked him very quietly if he was serious. Because if he was, then I would be available for the Christmas disco at a price to be negotiated.'

'Sandra! What did he say?'

'Nothing at first. Then he smiled. I think it was a smile. And said, "Miss Adams, I think we can do business..."'

Sandra shook her head sadly. 'But it looks like my garlic crushers are going to be redundant. Hayley will have let the cat out of the bag by now.'

But, as school ended for the day, Mel still wasn't sure whether Hayley had or she hadn't. She certainly wasn't talking to Mel, but then she appeared not to be talking to Darren Hogg either. She just swept furiously out of class, leaving him looking mystified.

Had 'the parcel delivered' an ultimatum? Was Darren Hogg going to miss the last post? By the way he was looking through his bag it definitely looked like he was missing something.

So – did the boys know that they knew what they were up to?

What exactly was going on?

*

Robbie was wishing he was somewhere else as they settled themselves in Zygs' for Twilly's ritual of the *Snogathon* progress meeting.

He didn't seem to be the only one, either. Daz had a permanent frown on his face as he dipped repeatedly into his bag. He hardly looked at the score-sheet as it was passed round. Even the sight of his name up there at the top of the list didn't stir him.

1. Hogg, D.	2,265
2. Morris, G.	2,244
3. Brookes, R.	1,308
4. Atwill, M.	300

'What's up, Daz?' chortled Greg. 'Hayley given you the big E, has she?'

'Shut your face.'

'Charming! If he's like this when he's ahead, what's he going to be like when I overtake him?'

'If you overtake me,' growled Daz.

'*When* I overtake you,' repeated Greg. 'With twenty-two seconds unused, I've still got near enough four hundred more credits I can clock up with Purity, and over three weeks to do it in. So –' He looked round the table with his hand out, 'if you three want to concede defeat and give me the money now...'

'The *Snogathon* ends at the Christmas disco and not before,' said Twilly firmly.

Greg couldn't resist it. 'Why's that, Twilly? Going to make your big bid for glory then, are you? Come through at the gallop and win by a long nose, or whatever they call it?'

'Short head,' said Twilly, calmly.

Greg shrugged. 'Short head, big head, who cares. Admit it, lads, this race is as good as over. That is unless

Brookesie's planning another pop at Micro?'

Robbie shook his head. 'No, I'm not. Now puff off. I want to find out how Mr Zyg's getting on.'

When they'd gone, Robbie had a chat with Mrs Zyg. She said Mr Zyg was much the same. He'd had more tests and they all showed it was going to be a long job.

'Well, give him my best,' he said.

'Why you not give it him yourself?' asked Mrs Zyg. 'Come with me tomorrow, Robbie. I know he love to see you.'

The cat wasn't out of the bag at all. Something was, but it wasn't a cat – as Mel discovered immediately a sour-faced Hayley had led her and Sandra into the girls' loos, into the second cubicle from the left for extra security, then clanged the door shut.

'Daz,' she snapped. 'I've given him up.'

'Pity,' said Sandra. 'We could have made life very nasty for him. But you admit we were right, then?'

Hayley waved an irritated hand. 'I don't know. I never got to him. Straight after I left you I met Greg. He smarmed up alongside me and said, "I know we aren't together any more, Hayley, but you're still very special to me and I don't think what Daz is doing is right, not considering he's supposed to be er...concentrating on you. But that's for you to decide. Here." And he handed me – this!'

'This' was a dog-eared notebook which, lip curled in disgust, she pulled from inside her blouse and slapped on the cistern.

Mel opened it at the first page. Carmichael's Wordsworth quotation was at the top, but that was the one and only link with the poetry they'd been covering. Which wasn't to say that the book didn't contain any poetry. It did. Verses and verses of it. And all drawn from the same abundant source of inspiration, Mel realised as she read the first (and only non-pornographic) verse:

I dreamed of Ms Weston
Without any vest on.
We went to the wood –
It wasn't half good!

'The unfaithful swine!' wailed Hayley. 'Writing a poem all about her! What's Ms Weston got that I haven't?'

'You want that in round numbers?' sighed Sandra.

Hayley's chin wobbled. 'There's only one place for this!' she cried, snatching up Darren Hogg's log-book. She would have thrown it down the pan and pulled the chain if Mel hadn't moved quickly to yank it out of her hand.

'You're right, Hay,' she said. 'There *is* only one place for this. And I know just where it is...'

*

Robbie perched himself on a chair near the end of Mr Zyg's bed. On the other side sat Mrs Zyg, her small hands cradling one of her husband's.

Different company was good for Mr Zyg, she'd told Robbie. After a stroke it was a case of the brain learning how to do things again. It was like Mr Zyg had gone part-way back to being a baby, so he'd got to re-learn how to move his arms and legs and talk and everything. And when it came to the talking bit, hearing lots of different people talk to him was like a bottle of medicine.

In which case, thought Robbie, *Mrs Zyg must count as a barrel or two!*

She'd hardly stopped talking, nattering on and on about the shop and different customers. Then a nurse turned up and said the doctor would like a word with her. Off she went, leaving Robbie alone with Mr Zyg.

He was propped up on a mountain of pillows, wearing striped pyjamas. He'd changed. It looked to Robbie as if half of the burly man had died. He was able to raise his right hand a little way, but his left couldn't move. Same with his left leg. And when he tried to speak, all he could manage was a gurgle.

Robbie didn't know what to say. It was like facing one of those deadly talks teachers made them do in front of the class sometimes – not so bad for the first thirty seconds, but after that you know you're going to be struggling.

Then he remembered what Mrs Zyg had told him on the way there. 'Don't you worry what to say, Robbie. It not matter. As long my Zygmunt hearing plenty of words, that the important thing.'

You need Carmichael, then! thought Robbie. *He's the boy for words. Not to mention Wordsworth!*

Whether that was what gave him the idea of reading to Mr Zyg, he didn't know. But that's how he got started. Flipping open his bag, he pulled out the photocopied page Carmichael had handed him as they'd passed in the corridor.

'Thought you might like this, Mr Brookes.'

'Thanks,' he'd said.

'No,' Carmichael had added mysteriously, 'thank *you*, Mr Brookes.'

Quietly at first, then with more volume as Mr Zyg's eyes flicked his way, Robbie began to read aloud.

'Music, when soft voices die,
Vibrates in the memory…'

Mr Zyg seemed to enjoy it, kind of nodding as he finished. Encouraged, Robbie started talking.

'You know who wrote that don't you, Mr Zyg? Bloke called Shelley. Percy Bysshe Shelley. What a name, eh? No wonder he got picked on at school! Mind you, the girls didn't pick on him. Well, they did, but in a different way. Did you know he ran off to Scotland with a sixteen-year-old? Yep, married her he did. Two kids. Didn't stop him leaving her and running off with another sixteen-year-old later on, though!'

Mr Zyg could hear him, Robbie knew he could. He was pretty sure he was trying to laugh as well. His mouth was twitching at the corners and he was making a noise like a drain.

'Old Shelley was a bit different to you and Mrs Zyg, wasn't he Mr Zyg? I reckon you'd have liked him, though. I mean, he'd have been a racing cert for a copy of *Starkers!* every month, wouldn't he!'

*

Friday 27th November

Emotion: guilt.

In spite of all I've said recently about Carmichael, this log has served a useful purpose. It's given me a place where I could say what I feel without being afraid of offending anybody. It's been like a secret emotional diary. That's the reason I'm returning to it now. I've got a guilty secret. Darren Hogg has been suspended and it's all my fault!

*

Mel hadn't meant it to happen. Having got hold of Darren's book of erotic rhymes, her plan had been to plant it where it would cause him maximum humiliation – namely, in Ms Weston's post tray.

She'd slid it in there first thing that morning. But from then on, to her horror, the day had proceeded like there was some kind of mounting international crisis with developments every hour on the hour.

10.00 a.m. Darren was unceremoniously hauled out of History by a puce-faced Ms Weston looking like her whole being was about to burst, as opposed to just the usual part of her anatomy.

11.00 a.m. Darren's locker was raided and all his books carted off to some unknown destination.

12 noon. Mrs Hogg was seen driving into the school car park alone followed, shortly after, by Mrs Hogg being seen driving out of the school car park – this time with Darren slumped in the passenger seat.

1.00 p.m. Afternoon registration. Ms Weston issued a bulletin. 'Darren Hogg has been sent home. He has been interviewed by the Head and has admitted being the author of a foul and lewd document. He will not be allowed to return to school until a full investigation has taken place.'

Mel had looked at Sandra. Sandra had looked at

Hayley. Hayley had looked at Greg Morris. Greg Morris had looked pleased.

2.00 p.m. 'Act innocent,' hissed Sandra as they got ready for Games.

'Don't you feel guilty?' asked Mel.

'Be serious, Mel,' said Hayley triumphantly.

3.00 p.m. Sandra demonstrated exactly what she meant. Innocently she asked Ms Weston, 'What *was* in Darren Hogg's book, Miss?'

'A disgusting poem, she was told. Full of personal comments about a...a member of the teaching staff.'

Mel had tried to make a plea for clemency without making it look like she was making a plea for clemency. 'They're at that age, though, aren't they, Ms Weston? They'll grow out of it, I reckon. Perhaps you – I mean, whoever Darren wrote about – should look on it as a compliment.'

Ms Weston turned purple. 'You cannot be serious, Melanie! This is a matter of respect! If boys don't learn to respect females at this age, they never will!'

Or is it all my fault? Ms Weston's right. It is all about respect, isn't it? I didn't write that poem, did I? All I did was bring it to a wider audience (and they don't come much wider than Ms Weston!) Why should I feel guilty?

Emotion: ~~guilt~~ innocence!

*

Robbie spent Sunday afternoon at the hospital.

Mr Zyg still couldn't say much, and when he tried it came out as a mix of gurgle and dribble that Mrs Zyg never seemed to tire of wiping away with a tissue.

So, Robbie noticed, Mr Zyg had started talking to her with his eyes. He would look at her, and she would look at him, and it was like they were having this great conversation without words.

And he found himself wondering whether the OM had ever tried having a decent conversation with his mum – with or without words.

As he got in, the phone was ringing. It was his mum. During their daily chats he'd always tried not to sound upset, make out he was managing, all AOK. This time though, after giving her an update on Mr Zyg, he couldn't hold it in.

'Come home soon, Mum. Please!'

'I'm not sure if I can, Robbie,' she said. 'Look, it'll be Christmas soon. You'll be able to come up here and stay for a while.'

'There's ages to go till Christmas. Why can't you come home?'

'Because…I can't. Not yet. Look, I've got to go. I don't know what Gran's phone bill will be…'

Only when she'd hung up had the OM wandered out of the lounge, a lager in his hand. Robbie was surprised. When he'd beaten him to the phone before, the OM had snatched it away and started yelling in one combined movement.

'It was Mum,' he said. 'I didn't know you were here. Did you want to talk to her?'

Robbie's dad shook his fuzzy head and slurred, 'Got nothing more to say to her, have I? Said it all. Told her my little fling's over. Told her it didn't mean anything. Told her I still love her. What else is there?'

It was pathetic. After seeing the way the Zygs were coping, to come home to this flash nothing was too much.

'How about telling her you're sorry, Dad?' Robbie shouted at the top of his voice. 'How about that?'

Twelfth Week of Term
Writing it Down

Monday 30th November
Emotion: guilt.

This time I don't think I'm going to change my mind. Dave Carmichael has been suspended, and guilty is how I really feel.

Puffin' hell! No English lesson! No Carmichael!

The rumours had been sweeping the school all morning, getting more and more fantastic as they went along.

Mr Carmichael had been having a clandestine affair with a girl in the Sixth Form.

Mr Carmichael had been having a clandestine affair with Ms Weston.

Mr Carmichael had been having a clandestine affair with Ms Weston, *every* girl in the Sixth Form and the dinner lady well known for her generous helpings.

Finally, the truth came out. During his interrogation by the Head, Daz had tried to shift the blame by saying he'd never have written what he had if Mr Carmichael hadn't given him the log-book in the first place and insisted they write down their innermost thoughts and emotions and he was sorry but he couldn't help it if his innermost thoughts and emotions always seemed to feature Ms Weston in a starring role.

On the credit side, Daz had apparently also told them that Carmichael had said anything they wrote would be private, for their eyes alone, and no way would he have recorded his innermost thoughts and emotions about Ms Weston's qualities if he'd known they'd later be seen by her and blown up out of all proportion, the thoughts and emotions, that is, not Ms Weston's qualities.

'Private? For your eyes alone?' the Head was supposed to have growled. 'We'll see about that.'

Which was where Daz's interrogation had ended. The next thing he'd known he was on the way home and, presumably, Carmichael had been taking his place in the hot seat.

*

It sure gave Robbie something different to talk to Mr Zyg about that evening.

'Our English teacher's been suspended because he got us to write about our emotions in a log-book and one of my mates wrote a rude poem – well, more of a rude epic – about one of our teachers, one with bazookas the size of cannonballs!'

Mr Zyg made a sound like he was gargling, but

Robbie could see his eyes were bellowing with laughter.

'Anyway, the teacher's not allowed in again till he faces a firing squad or disciplinary panel or something,' said Robbie, only to be surprised to hear himself add, 'but if you ask me, it's not right. I mean, he didn't do anything wrong, did he? Just got us to look at things more carefully and think about life a bit more.'

Mr Zyg's head fell forward on his chest. That was nothing new, he'd got a long way to go before he'd regain control over the muscles that keep it up.

'Puffin' hell,' Robbie went on, 'he even got me at it, and that's something! If anyone had told me at the start of term I'd be sat here reading poems to you and enjoying it, I'd have told them to get their heads looked at!'

He'd pulled out a book, ready to start reading another poem or two to Mr Zyg, when he realised there was no point. He'd fallen asleep.

Robbie knew Mrs Zyg wouldn't be ready to go yet. She was with some white coats arguing about arrangements for taking her husband home again. He dipped into the flat pocket at the bottom of his school bag to check his Carmichael log-book was there. After the near miss with Mel Bradshaw and the *Snogathon* rules, and now Daz, he'd decided this was a book he wanted in a safe place.

He pulled it out. *Maybe Mr Zyg would like to hear a bit of* Snogathon *detail when he wakes up!*

Robbie slowly flipped over the pages, glancing up at Mr Zyg as he did so. *Poor bloke. Does he feel as bad as he looks?* Robbie started doodling…

> He slumps in his bed,
> Hardly moving at all…

He stopped suddenly, staring at the page. He'd written the opening lines of a poem. Of sound mind, and of his own free will, Robbie Brookes had started writing a puffin' poem!

*

Wednesday 2nd December

Reactions to the DC situation have been mixed. Sandra's not fussed - teachers are like buses, there'll be another one along in a minute. Hayley's even less bothered - 'I didn't like him, too clever, he made me feel a dimmie.'

And what about me? How do I feel about the DC situation? Answer - worse.

Emotion: guiltier.

Why? Because I've spoken to him - and found out the truth.

It had happened at the end of the day. Mel had spotted him gliding in the back way as everybody else was heading out the front. She'd followed him up to his corner in the English Department and watched him scoop papers together, uncertain of what to say, or even why she wanted to say anything.

But when he pulled the handwritten 'How Do I Love Thee?' poem from under its magnet and dropped it into the bin, she just had to say something.

'Mr Carmichael?'

'Miss Bradshaw. Melanie. Hello.'

'I...I just wanted to say I'm sorry about what happened. It was partly my fault Ms Weston found that book.'

'Really? Don't worry about it. "He is all fault who hath no fault at all", and I'm sure the poet Tennyson would have changed his opening word to "She" if you'd asked him nicely. Now if you'll excuse me, I'd better get moving. I'm not supposed to be here.'

Gathering a few more books and papers into his arms he followed Mel out into the corridor and closed the door behind him.

'When will you be coming back?' she asked.

'That depends on the Governors. Soon, I hope.'

'Can they sack you?'

Carmichael smiled. *Nice smile*, thought Mel. *Sort of older-brotherly.*

'I don't think they will,' he said, 'but it's possible. In which case I'll try to see it as another test of my renewed hope about life following death – as championed by your Mr Brookes.'

What he'd said took a second to register. When it did, Mel let him know it. 'He's not *my* Mr Brookes!'

An apologetic hand shot up. 'Now it's my turn to say sorry,' said the teacher. 'A poor choice of words. Of course I should have said "as championed by your *poetry partner*, Mr Brookes".'

Mel felt like telling him she wished Robbie Brookes had never been that either, but it didn't seem the moment.

'I was referring to the other day,' Dave Carmichael went on. 'When he asked about the poem by Shelley. You remember it?'

She nodded. '"Music, when soft voices die, vibrates in the memory". Lines like that are hard to forget.'

'Well, they helped me a lot. I'd been feeling very sorry for myself.' Mel could tell he wasn't sure whether to say more – but he did. 'A person who meant a great deal to me walked out of my life a few weeks ago. Just before half-term.'

The source of the handwritten 'How Do I Love Thee?'

she'd just seen him throw away? It had to be!

'I thought it was the end of the world,' sighed Carmichael. 'I spent the whole of half-term week in a... well, let's just say I took a leaf out of Coleridge's book.'

He didn't have to spell it out. Mel remembered the private lives of poets lesson well enough. *Samuel Taylor Coleridge was usually roaring drunk.*

Mel gulped. *He'd been drowning his sorrows. Reflecting on his powerful feelings in tranquillity – except that it had been the bottle that had been overflowing.*

'When we came back after half-term I just went through the motions – until, as I say, Mr Brookes reminded me of Shelley's poem. That day made all the difference. It reminded me that life goes on. So, hold on to the good memories, but leave the rest of the garbage behind, that's the message, Miss Bradshaw! That's what would shine out from my log-book if I'd been keeping one.' He raised an eyebrow. 'Have you been keeping yours?'

Mel gulped. Words stuck in her throat. Finally she managed, 'Yes. It's been...useful.'

'Good.' The teacher chuckled loudly. 'Mr Hogg obviously thought so too, even if Ms Weston wasn't impressed with the results!'

'You don't regret doing it, then?'

Dave Carmichael shook his head and his brown hair flopped in the way Mel had found so knee-knockingly attractive when he first arrived.

'Not for a minute. I don't even regret paying for those books out of my own pocket.' He lowered his voice. 'Because, between you and me, Melanie, reading Mr Hogg's epic was worth every penny!'

Still chuckling, he strode down the corridor, papers flapping under his arm and a spring in his step.

Thursday 3rd December

Have I got it all wrong?

Are the male species really kind and considerate under the skin? If you scratch a boy, will you always find a warm, generous, sensible human being underneath?

Maybe it's just a case of having to scratch some harder than others. Maybe, metaphorically speaking, some just need a quick scrape with a fingernail while others take a steady gouging with a chain saw.

Or is Dave Carmichael an exception to the rule that says 'Show me a male and I'll show you a self-centred clown'?

Emotion: confused.

The numbers voting for DC being an exception to the

rule were mounting steadily. Once it would have been just Mel and Sandra. Hayley had since seen it their way, of course. And now Purity Meek had been converted!

Working separately, Sandra and Hayley had been planting seeds of doubt in her mind about Greg Morris. Those seeds, Mel discovered in the girls' loos the next day, had just germinated.

'You were right,' barked Purity. 'Bleedin' caught him at it yesterday evening, didn't I? In a shop doorway we was. Regular stop when we're out mooching it is and me, silly cow, never thinks to ask why it's the same shop doorway every time.'

Angrily stubbing out her cigarette on the side of a sink, Purity squashed the remains down the plug-hole, sluiced it away, then went back to her story.

'Jewellers, ennit? Window full of clocks. There we are, snoggin' merrily, but when I open one eye what's he doing? Watching the second hand on a chiming wall clock with hourly strike and quartz pendulum bleedin' movement!'

'Credit where it's due, Purity,' giggled Mel. 'You can't beat quartz for accuracy.'

'Accuracy? I'll give him bleedin' accuracy. I all but kneed him in the nuts when I saw him at it, but I stopped meself just in time. No, Purity, I said, remember what Sandra and Hayley said. Humiliation. That's what he deserves. And that's what he's going to get Saturday afternoon.'

'Where?' asked Hayley, wide-eyed.

'Lovers' Bench. Told him I'd be walking my dog near there, nudge nudge wink wink.'

'And he fell for it?' asked Mel.

'Like a lamb to the bleedin' slaughter,' cackled Purity.

*

What an end to the week! thought Robbie. He'd just been hit by two invitations – one bad, and one so bad that it made the first seem positively pleasant.

The first invitation had been from Greg. 'Witnessing duties, Brookesie. Lovers' Bench, tomorrow at half-two.' He smirked his finest smirk. 'You'll be able to say you were there when the *Snogathon* champion made sure of his title.'

Robbie was still feeling low about that prospect when Ms Weston bustled in late to their tutorial. The news she broke simply didn't compare.

'I have an important message from the Head,' she said, flapping a sheet of notepaper bearing the school crest. 'It reads as follows. "To aid the deliberations of the disciplinary panel considering the teaching of English to this group, you are all required to hand in the log-books Mr Carmichael gave you –"' she ignored the

bursts of protest and finished what she had to say.
'" – by 3 p.m. on Monday!'

*

Was there a nice literary word for 'up yours, mate!'? Because if there was, that's the one Robbie wanted.

He was not handing his log-book in, no way. They could do what they liked, stick him on a pitchfork and grill him till he was well done on both sides, but his book was staying private.

Looking back over the pages, he reckoned it had been good for him. It showed he'd changed. Not much, but some. His first entries had made him seem a bit flash. OK, very flash. It wasn't hard to see why Mel Bradshaw had turned her nose up at him.

Pity, though. If things had worked out differently with her he could have been way ahead in the *Snogathon* by now. On the other hand, maybe he should think himself lucky. If Mel had actually read that rules and tariffs sheet, instead of giving it straight back to him none the wiser, he'd have been the one with his nose turned up – by Mel's fist!

As it was, Greg looked more than ever like a sure-fire winner. Especially now. A Saturday-afternoon invitation to meet Purity Meek on the Lovers' Bench?

Puffin' hell, if Greg didn't hit maximum today, he'd be as sick as a pig...

Saturday 5th December

   Emotion: euphoria!

   Revenge is sweet. But being there to see it happen is even sweeter!

The girls had met at the park gates and scurried round to a prime position behind the far corner of the beech hedge surrounding the bowling green.

Leaning out, Sandra Adams trained her eighty-magnification zoom binoculars on the Lovers' Bench and began a running commentary.

'Here comes Purity. Morris's sitting there, licking his lips. Purity's tying her dog to the bench. Now she's sitting down. He's sliding towards her. She's smiling invitingly. He's grinning like it's his birthday. He's putting his arm round her. He's zooming in. Oh, it's perfect!'

'What is?' cried Mel.

'He's got his mouth open! He's after a Frenchie! Purity's got her teeth clenched, though. She's holding him off while she slides her hand round the back of his neck. Now the other hand. She's locking her fingers together! Brilliant, Purity! Morris is stuck now! A small tank couldn't break out of that grip!'

'Come on, Purity,' breathed Hayley.

'Here we go. She's given Morris a green-light smile. He's opened his gob even wider. You could fit a Big Mac in there sideways! He's closing in! Purity's opening her mouth at last. Go, girl, go!'

From their hiding place amongst the large rhododendron bushes which arced around behind the Lovers' Bench, Robbie and Malcolm Atwill watched what happened next with amazement.

The moment the two shapes on the bench merged into one, Twilly started his watch. But, almost at once, half the shape started impersonating a bucking bronco and trying to go back the way it had come. Greg's half.

Unbelievably, he was giving every impression of not wanting the snog to last for six seconds, let alone sixty. It seemed to Robbie as if he was trying to lean back, push Purity off, and beg for mercy all at the same time. But Purity clearly wasn't going to let him go. She had Greg in a head-lock that he couldn't break...

Twilly counted until the minute was up. '...fifty-nine, sixty!'

On the Lovers' Bench, almost as if she'd been counting herself, Purity finally let Greg out of her clutches. It was like a champagne cork being released from its bottle. As Purity smiled, untied her dog and trotted cheerfully off in the direction of the bowling green, Greg leaped from the bench and hared for the bushes.

He was still throwing up when they got to him. 'That's it,' he moaned, 'end of the line. That dog had fresher breath than her!'

Behind the beech hedge Mel, Sandra and Hayley were in hysterics.

'Ye-ess!' they hooted when Purity rounded the corner, unwrapping multiple sticks of spearmint chewing gum and stuffing them into her mouth like a squirrel stocking up for the winter.

'Brilliant,' cried Mel. 'What on earth did you eat before you got here?'

Purity cackled. 'A slab of garlic bread and half a jar of pickled onions. Bleedin' lovely!'

*

Mr Zyg had been allowed home. The white coats weren't that keen, but Mrs Zyg had pushed them. 'You want my Zygmunt to remember? Then I take him home. That is where all his memories are!'

So instead of reading Mr Zyg poems in a hospital ward, Robbie went to the little house two streets away from the shop and read to him there. It was better. Mrs Zyg could come and go as she liked, and Mr Zyg looked happier even though his speech was still bad and there were long spells when he gave Robbie the impression he didn't know what was going on at all.

'Is long job, Robbie,' says Mrs Zyg, brushing her hand

across Mr Zyg's lolling head as she came in to discover that he'd fallen asleep in the middle of a bit of Coleridge's 'The Ancient Mariner'. 'You doing him good. And me. Read some more for me...'

I noticed something at the Zygs'. While I was reading, Mrs Zyg sat there, holding Mr Zyg's hand and just gazing at him. It was as if she could see something that nobody else can, like the way she saw something different in him that first time they met. She had a little smile on her face – like the babe in that famous painting.

I expect Carmichael knows the one. He knows a lot of stuff. I hope some of it helps him when he faces the firing squad. I hope he gets off, too.

Robbie looked at the entry he'd just logged. *Sad, or what!*

No, it wasn't. It was what he felt. Anyway, nobody would ever see it. Like old Carmichael had said, his log-book was private...and it was staying that way!

Thirteenth Week of Term

Keeping Mum

Making good her Friday threat, Chesty Weston marched into registration and demanded their Carmichael logbooks.

Around her, Mel was aware of some slow digging into bags. She didn't look to see who was digging and who wasn't. She was bracing herself for a solo display of defiance. Standing up, she coughed loudly.

'When Mr Carmichael gave us those books he promised that nobody else would see them.'

Ms Weston sniffed. 'Then he was mistaken. The Head wishes to read your book, Melanie, and if the Head wishes to read your book then the Head will read your book.'

Mel appealed to her sense of humour. 'Why? To see if I've written any poems like, er… "I dreamt of the Head, snoring in bed"? Believe me, I haven't. Taking my book in can only be a big disappointment.'

But Ms Weston's reaction only left Mel thinking that if there was a biological link between sense of humour and bust size, then she didn't want her bits growing any more. Her tutor hadn't even cracked her face, just said a word at a time, 'Melanie – you – will – hand – in – your – book!'

She'd left her no alternative. 'Sorry, I won't,' said Mel.

'You will! The Head demands it!'

It was then that support came galloping over the hill from a totally unexpected direction.

'Tough,' called Robbie, leaping to his feet. 'Don't give your log in if you don't want to, Mel. They're not getting mine, either.'

Phew! Refusing to hand over his log-book hadn't been easy, what with Chesty looking ready to spurt flame from her nostrils, but Mel had made it a lot easier. It had earned him a smile from her, too!

'What is this, a revolution?' snapped Chesty, swinging round on Robbie like a twin-turret tank.

She wasn't wrong. A swell of defiance was now bubbling up. And, Robbie was relieved to see, Twilly was joining it. If he was to hand in the *Snog Log*, there'd be another three of them following Daz out of the front gates!

'Er...I'm afraid mine has suffered a tragic accident, Ms Weston,' said Twilly. 'It's been burnt.'

'Malcolm Atwill, you don't live in a house with an open fire. Your father spent the whole of last parents' evening advising me about gas central heating.'

Twilly didn't bat an eyelid. 'But the radiators get very hot, Miss.'

By now, the whole group was on its feet. Ms Weston was going purple, hardly knowing what to say to quell their rebellion.

'You are being very silly!' she screeched. 'The Head wishes to inspect these books. They are the property of the school!'

It was Mel's big moment. With her heart pounding like a disco beat she said firmly, 'They're not, actually.'

Ms Weston turned her glare onto full beam. 'Melanie Bradshaw,' she said as if addressing an infant, 'every item of educational apparatus you are given in this school is paid for out of the public purse.'

Mel was inspired. 'Well those log-books weren't. They were paid for out of Mr Carmichael's purse. He told me so himself.'

'What?'

'Mr Carmichael bought them out of his own money, Ms Weston,' said Mel. She felt a final surge of courage. 'So if we have to give them to anybody it should be him.'

Robbie punched the air. 'And he said he'd never want to see them!' he yelled. 'Checkmate!'

And that was it. Well, almost. After Ms Weston had rumbled away, muttering, 'I am going to talk to the

Head!' making it sound to Robbie like it was a spare one she kept in a box at home, Mel drifted his way.

'Thanks for helping out,' she said.

He shrugged. 'That's what enemies are for.' She gave him an encouraging kind of smile.

Could it be a Mr Zyg moment? he wondered. *Another chance to apologise? Only one way to find out.*

'You never did let me say sorry for not turning up that time...' he said.

Sorry? Mel was surprised that any boy would have the word in his vocabulary, let alone R. Brookes. What could she say? *No problem, Robbie. I'd have been sorrier if you had turned up?* Not after he'd supported her the way he had.

'I had a good reason, y'know,' she heard him add.

'Tricycle broke down, did it?' quipped Mel before she could stop herself. She felt a pang of shame.

'No,' said Robbie. 'Mr Zyg. He runs a paper shop. I was there when he broke down – well, had a stroke. I helped take him to hospital. By the time I got out...'

'Too late, right?' asked Mel.

He's looking sorry, she thought, *but is he? Is he really?* She couldn't allow herself to be fooled. This was a boy who'd got her down as a good points-scorer in their grubby *Snogathon*. So, he'd helped this Mr Zyg. A one-off emergency situation, probably. But then again, he'd just helped her as well...

It was all getting too complicated. Was she supposed to detest Robbie Brookes or not? Why did he have to make things difficult by being nice? Typical!

Mel changed the subject, fast. 'What do you think'll happen to Mr Carmichael? Get the sack?'

'I don't see why he should,' said Robbie. 'I mean, Chesty wasn't meant to see what Daz wrote, and Carmichael didn't actually *make* us write anything, did he? Just suggested we noticed things and wrote about our...' He felt his face flush. '...y'know, feelings and stuff.'

Mel couldn't believe it. He was embarrassed. Beneath his big-I-am exterior, Robbie Brookes was – what? Normal? Likeable?

'And did you?' she asked, surprised that she actually wanted to know the answer. 'Write about your, y'know, feelings and stuff?'

'Yeah,' said Robbie. 'Did you?'

He wasn't supposed to ask that! This time it was Mel who felt herself going all shades of crimson. 'Sometimes,' she said. 'In an odd moment. Just the occasional snippet.'

Do not ask me what I wrote about! she thought. *Don't even think about it!*

But he clearly wasn't. Robbie Brookes, class

comedian, simply said, 'Stunner, eh? Carmichael must have something going for him to get me doing that,' before drifting away and leaving her feeling totally confused.

Robbie Brookes reckons DC is a goodie? So where does that leave me? Do I hate DC or not? Do I loathe Robbie Brookes or not?

She found herself calling after him. 'So what are you going to do? Are you going to let them see your book if they insist?'

'No way!' shouted Robbie.

Reality bubbled back to the surface, then. Of course he wasn't going to hand his log-book in. Because it was crammed full of grubby *Snogathon* details, the dirty devil, that was why!

Yes, I do. I hate Robbie Brookes! Definitely. Certainly. Probably. Maybe. I think.

*

Victory was theirs!

A sour Ms Weston broke the news to them through gritted teeth in registration the following morning. They could hand in their log-books anonymously – and voluntarily! If they chose to hang on to them, they weren't allowed to bring them into school. If they did they'd be treated in the same way as hand-held games and mobile phones – confiscated at once. (And only returned after the staff have finished using them! thought Robbie.)

He told Mr Zyg all about it when he visited him after school to give Mrs Zyg a chance to make sure her new shop assistant helper was coping all right.

'I never imagined I'd say this about Chesty,' said Robbie, 'but when she broke the news she looked really deflated!'

He saw the familiar laughing twinkle zip into Mr Zyg's eyes, his lips lengthening in a lopsided smile. But it didn't last. After another couple of minutes the big man's head was lolling onto his chest and he'd nodded off.

Robbie studied him, remembering the way he was before his stroke. Then he tried to conjure up a picture of how he must have looked when Mrs Zyg first met him. It was hard. Nowadays, awake or asleep, Mr Zyg looked pretty much the same. Robbie turned again to his doodle poem, now a bit longer...

He slumps in his bed,
Hardly moving at all.
His face is a blank,
Just like a brick wall.
His laugh is no more,
Nor his bellowing call...

He doodled on. By the time Mrs Zyg breezed in half an hour later, he'd finished.

'What you write, Robbie?' she asked.

'Ah, nothing. Just messing about.'

'Well you keep doing it. Zygmunt like you to come. I can tell. Hey, and you tell your teacher I say so.'

'Right, I will. When I see him.'

If I see him, more like, thought Robbie. *If he doesn't get the bullet.*

Carmichael's court martial had to be coming up soon. Maybe he should get Mrs Zyg to write the judges a note: *This teacher he must be okey-dokey. He teach Robbie Brookes about poetry and emotions and stuff. He should get the medals, not the bullets!*

*

The idea came out of nowhere.

Maybe it was what Mrs Zyg had said, or maybe it was him thinking about her imaginary note. Maybe it was a touch of Carmichael-type inspiration! Whatever. Robbie decided to do it.

Sticking a copy of his poem about Mr Zyg into an envelope, he scribbled out a short note:

Dear Sir/Madam

Mr Carmichael is OK. It's not his fault Darren wrote what he did. At least Mr Carmichael tried

something different and you can't blame him
for that.

Yours faithfully – Robbie Brookes, Year 9

He thought briefly about adding that neither was it
Daz's fault if Chesty had got a front that turned corners
five minutes before the rest of her, but decided against
it. If Daz had only written a couple of verses it might
have been different, but 216 searing stanzas was
definitely over the top, to coin a phrase.

What he did add was this:

P.S. Enclosed is a poem I wrote about a good man I
know. I'd never even have started it without
Mr Carmichael's inspiration.

Then he dropped it off with the School Secretary. It
wasn't much, but it was the best he could do.

*

Preparations for the Christmas disco had begun in
earnest. The school hall was being decorated. Tinsel had
begun to sprout from the most unlikely places and
herds of reindeer with luminous noses were galloping
across the walls. And, as Mel saw when she peered in,
something round was now dangling from the ceiling.

'Take a good look at that,' said Sandra, rushing up to

her with a gleam in her eye and Hayley in tow. 'That's the ultimate humiliation, that is.'

'It looks more like a knobbly football, Sandra,' laughed Mel.

'No it's not,' said Hayley. 'It's a camera. Like they have in the clothes shops to make sure you're not walking off with a jumper up your jumper.'

'I've been talking to the Year 11 pus-factory who's in charge of it,' said Sandra. 'The organising committee have really gone to town on the hi-tech stuff this year. They're going to take pictures with that camera and show them on a big screen.'

'So people can be seen dancing!' cried Hayley.

'So people can be seen doing anything,' said Sandra, adding pointedly, 'or be seen having anything done to them.' She looped her arm in Mel's and led her off down the corridor.

'That ceiling camera isn't the only one they've got,' murmured Sandra as they walked. 'There'll be a roving camera as well. Another of the Year 11's will be prowling round with it. I spent yesterday discussing exposures with him.'

'Sandra,' laughed Mel, 'have you no shame?'

'Be serious, Mel!' snapped Sandra. 'Don't you see? It's perfect for completing Mission Revenge! What could be more humiliating for Malcolm Atwill than for me to manoeuvre him into an embarrassing position, then have that camera leap out so that his agonies are blown up and splattered in all their wide-screen glory for the whole world to see!'

Nothing could be more humiliating, Mel agreed. Her only question concerned which aspect of Malcolm Atwill exactly did Sandra plan to blow up and splatter?

'What have you got cooking in that nasty mind of yours?' she asked.

'Cooking, Mel? You must be clairvoyant!' Sandra didn't explain why, just went on, 'Think. Malcolm Atwill is planning on getting me in a dark corner so that he can grit his teeth, close his eyes, hold his nose, and kiss me for long enough to win that *Snogathon* money. Right?'

Mel gaped at her. 'You mean you're going to let him? And have *that* flashed up on the screen?'

Sandra shook her head. 'Oh he'll be appearing as one half of a double act, all right. But not with me.'

'Then...who?'

'Who else do we want to humiliate, Mel? Robbie Brookes, of course! I've got it all worked out. What we have to do is arrange to meet them during the interval. In the cookery room.'

'The cook – why?'

'Because they'll fall for it when we say it's nice and

quiet. What they won't twig is the real reason – that it's got larder cupboards big enough to hide a roving cameraman, not to mention plentiful supplies of water and flour which we'll have loaded into pots and pans beforehand. It'll be the ice-rink humiliation scenario, only better, because it'll all be beamed onto the screen in the hall!'

Mel had got the picture. 'And you want me to entice Robbie Brookes along for the treatment, right?'

'Yep. You arrange to meet him a couple of minutes after the time I give Atwill. Then, when they're both inside...wham! Flour power! It'll be fantastic!'

*

Thursday 10th December

I can't fault Sandra's plan. It's going to be like an omnibus edition of The Surgeon or one of those film sequels. Revenge is Sweet 2.

All I have to do is sweet-talk Robbie Brookes into taking me to the Christmas disco, then get him into the cookery room - where he'll get his just desserts!

He's going to regret the day this Snogathon ever began!

Odd thought #1: I wonder what position he's in.

Odd thought #2: I wonder why he hasn't already asked me out again. Is it because he's miles in the lead - or miles behind?

Odd thought #3: For crying out loud, why am I even wondering these things?!

*

Saturday 12th December

Mum's back. My mum's home again.

There'd been no warning, not even a mention the last time Robbie had spoken to her on the phone. The taxi had just pulled up and out she'd climbed. Up the path with her suitcase, through the door and into the kitchen to put the kettle on as if she'd never been away.

Robbie had never felt so happy – and never seen the OM so gobsmacked. He looked as if he didn't know whether to jump up and down with joy or anger. In the end he just put his arms round her and mumbled something like, 'You should have said. I'd have tidied up a bit.'

For the rest of the day, the OM acted like a dog on a tight leash. He stayed in, didn't yell, helped with bits of housework – even called Mum 'darling' once!

Same goes for me, I suppose, thought Robbie. Hadn't he tidied his room, offered to make the tea, peel the spuds – even done the washing-up?

Mrs Brookes had wandered out while he was up to his elbows in soapsuds. She'd grabbed a tea-towel and started wiping. He hadn't known what to say. In the end he'd just come out with, 'I'm glad you're home, Mum. I...I thought you weren't coming back.'

'I thought I wasn't as well. Until...' She stopped in mid-stream.

'Until what?' asked Robbie, hopefully. 'Until Dad said sorry?'

'Say sorry? Your dad?'

His mum laughed. It was the most miserable laugh he'd ever heard. She shook her head. 'Oh, he finally said that all right. But whether he was sorry because of what he'd done, or sorry for being found out I'm not sure. Time will tell. No, hearing him say sorry helped, but that wasn't the main reason I came back.'

'What was, then?'

'Because I suddenly realised: I've done it. I've shown him I won't take it.'

She tossed the tea-towel over the rail. 'Yes, I've come back to him, Robbie. But he knows now I can just as easily go away again.'

Last Week of Term
Ending in Style

Carmichael was back, too. With everybody expecting another lacklustre hour in the company of Ms Supply Substitute, or whatever her name was, in he strolled.

'Ladies and gentlemen,' he smiled. 'I have good news and bad news. Which would you like first?'

'The bad news,' somebody called out.

'You're back,' said Greg, loudly.

Carmichael laughed. 'Half right, Mr Morris. Not bad, for you.' He waited for the hooting to fade, then said, 'Yes, I'm back. The bad news is that, as I understand it, Mr Hogg is excluded until the start of next term.'

Greg winked at Robbie. 'Aw. Sad,' he muttered.

'Still, at least we've both been forgiven,' said Carmichael. 'Surprised as I am.'

'Why?' Robbie found himself asking.

'Why am I surprised, Mr Brookes?' Carmichael hesitated. 'Because although I explained the purpose of having you all keep logs – to get you to thinking more deeply, etc. – I ended my interview with the distinct feeling that the disciplinary panel hadn't been convinced.'

He clapped his hands together, as if to declare the

whole matter at an end. 'But obviously I was wrong. So here I am, and here you are, and...' He waved a large thick poetry anthology above his head, 'here are another thousand poems I want to cover before the end of the school year, so let's crack on!'

*

Monday 14th December

Emotion: relief, relief and relief.

Relief that that whole business is over; relief that my role in planting Darren Hogg's log-book didn't lose Carmichael his job; and relief that I'm no longer besotted with him.

As he talked, I realised then that my deep desire to see him basted with oil and slowly barbecued had evaporated. But my previous and opposite desire, as revealed in these pages, hadn't returned! I was pleased for him, but only because he was pleased. That was it. I didn't see him as Mr Perfect any more. Just Mr Slightly-Imperfect.

Straight after English, 3.00 p.m.-3.02 p.m.

Emotion: uncertainty, uncertainty, uncertainty.

All three about Robbie Brookes and the Christmas disco.

Egged on by Sandra and Hayley, Mel had headed for

Robbie Brookes the moment the lesson ended. Dave Carmichael had left with a throwaway line about saving the poetry partner project until the start of next term, so she had the perfect excuse. What she didn't seem to have was the fired-up motivation.

'Just tempt him,' hissed Sandra. 'Make sure he'll be there, dreaming of scooping the *Snogathon* prize.'

Mel hesitated. 'I don't know, Sandra. I'm not sure he deserves this.'

'No, he deserves the garlic crushers like the rest of them. Compared to that, a couple of minutes' wide-screen humiliation will be nothing. Now, go on!'

Robbie smiled as she approached. Not the leer of the past, but a normal, friendly smile. 'Hi!' he said. 'Crisis over, eh?'

'Looks like it.'

Uncertainty, uncertainty, uncertainty!

'Er...do you want to talk about the poetry some time?' asked Mel.

'There's no hurry. Carmichael said he's saving it for next term.'

Should I, should I , should I?

'We could do it earlier. At...er...the Christmas disco. We could find a quiet corner.'

'To talk about poetry?'

Tempt, tempt, tempt!

'And other things, maybe. Ice-skating. Protest movements through the ages. Ms Weston. The state of the Icelandic economy. The sad decline of body-contact dancing.'

Robbie laughed. 'Me and you? At the Christmas disco? You're sure?'

Mel nodded. 'You and me? I'm positive.'

'Right. It's a date!'

*

Well, what do you know! Me and Melanie. Melanie and me. At the disco. Together. And she asked me!

Robbie was still well chuffed the next day as he shot off to the Zygs' shop straight after school. He had two reasons for going – only one of which was to tell Mrs Zyg he wouldn't be able to read to Mr Zyg that Thursday. The other was because Twilly had called for a final *Snogathon* review meeting.

'A disco!' beamed Mrs Zyg when he told her. 'Robbie, you the dancer like my Zygmunt, yah?'

'Head-banger, more like.'

'Bah! I bet the girls they think different. You going with a special?'

Robbie shrugged. 'Kind of. Her name's Mic...I mean, Melanie. She suggested we go together.'

Mrs Zyg beamed again. 'There you are, then! I bet she sees something different in you, like I first see in my Zygmunt!'

Robbie was about to bet her that Mr Zyg didn't flatten her toes like there was a good chance he'd do to Mel's when, just for a moment, her smile faded and she looked serious.

'I see something different in you recently, Robbie. You less the big-I-am. Is a good sign...'

She didn't get the chance to say any more because the door pinged open and in spilled the others. Daz was with them, phoned by Twilly to tell him about the meeting. Reluctantly, Robbie joined the group as they spread themselves round their usual table.

'In just over forty-eight hours, lads,' said Twilly, 'the Christmas disco will be under way. The final credit-scoring opportunity of the term. I take it nobody has any objections to using the one-witness rule again?' He didn't even bother to look up as he said, 'Good. And I'm sure that I don't need to remind you all that at the end of the evening the winner of the *Snogathon* will be decided.' He shuffled a sheet of paper round the table. 'Here is the current position.'

1. Morris, G.	2,640
2. Hogg, D.	2,265
3. Brookes, R.	1,308
4. Atwill, M	300

Daz scowled. 'Well there's puff-all I can do to change things. I'm not allowed into this disco.'

'You could disguise yourself,' said Greg, flippantly.

'Who as, Father puffin' Christmas? No, I concede. You're the winner.'

Greg nodded smugly. 'A piece of sound judgement, Dazzer. Which is why I will not be bothering to honour this event with my presence.'

Twilly gave him a withering look. 'That's the real reason, is it? Not because the word's gone round that you've got gut-rot and any babe going near you should wear a plastic mac in case you heave up all over them?'

'No it is not,' snapped Greg. 'It's a matter of simple mathematics. Daz is out and you two are miles behind. I'll stick on what I've got.'

'Is that your final word?' says Twilly, quickly and formally, 'you propose to retire with your current score?'

Greg walked straight into the trap. Because a trap it was.

'Yeah, yeah,' he said airily, 'I hereby declare on two thousand, six hundred and forty not out. Who's going to catch me anyhow?'

Twilly put his fingers together like a Mafia boss about to pass judgement on an underling who'd stepped out of line. 'Me,' he said.

'You!' exploded Greg, eyes popping. 'How? Bought a lorry-load of mistletoe, have you? Planning to get round the whole group in the evening, are you?'

'Not the whole group, no. Just one of them. Sandra Adams.'

'Amazon!' hooted Daz. 'She'll chew you up and spit you out in pieces!'

'Now that's where you're wrong,' said Twilly, coolly. 'Sandra and I have a – how can I put it? An arrangement. She's already agreed to come with me. And at her tariff of one hundred and fifty, all I need is to overtake Greg's score is…' he checked the figure he'd already calculated and jotted onto the notepad at his side, 'sixteen seconds.'

Greg was blazing. 'You've planned this all along! That's why you haven't been trying!'

Twilly smiled. 'Ever seen a poor bookmaker? Of course I planned it all along.' He rubbed his hands together. 'And in forty-eight hours, I'll be collecting.'

Greg swung round, pleading, 'Can't you stop him, Brookesie? Haven't you got anything lined up?'

Robbie hesitated. Should he mention Mel? He'd assumed Greg was going to be the winner, too. In fact the *Snogathon* had been out of his thinking for so long it felt as if he'd retired as well. But that was before hearing how Twilly had suckered them all.

Could he stop him? Mel was on a good tariff – quite good enough to overhaul Twilly if his mental arithmetic could be trusted. And weren't he and Mel now on the best of terms? Yes, everything was going his way. It had to be worth a crack. It had to be!

Wouldn't it just teach Twilly a lesson! He could just see the pained look on his mug when he had to hand over the prize money!

But no decent manager gave away his tactics to the opposition before a match, did he?

Robbie shook his head as he answered Greg's question. 'Nothing lined up at all, Gregso,' he said. 'Apart from witnessing for Twilly.'

*

Wednesday 16th December

Why doesn't it feel right?

Humiliation is no less than Robbie Brookes deserves, isn't it?

So, he's proved to be closer to a human being than I thought possible. But he's still a nasty boy, isn't he, thinking of me as a walking fund of snogathon points?

Yes, Sandra's right. As she's said often enough, if we get the chance of hitting one of them where it hurts then we should grab it with both hands!

Robbie had worked it out, confirming what his mental arithmetic had suspected.

Twilly & Amazon Adams:
16 secs at 150 - 2,400 plus current 300
= 2,700 credits.
Robbie & Melanie:
16 secs at 90 - 1,440 plus current 1,308
= 2,748 credits!
All I need is a tasty 16-second snogeroonee with Mel Bradshaw to beat Twilly by a nose!

*

Everything was ready.

The DJ was on stage, all flashing lights and glittering jacket. Suspended above it, and covering a good proportion of the hall's end wall, was a massive white screen.

Outside, the foyer had been turned into a refreshment area, with tables and chairs and a soft drinks bar. Robbie realised why, the moment the DJ let rip with his first play of the evening. The music was so loud it made the floor shake. Even Mr Zyg in his bellowing prime would have been drowned out. The foyer was for those who wanted to talk.

Robbie had been sitting on a chair with a good view of the entrance for the past ten minutes.

He'd seen Twilly arrive with Amazon, wearing what looked like his school shirt and trousers. His one concession to disco-dancing seemed to have been to leave his briefcase at home. Amazon, on the other hand, had been wearing a low-cut tent and flashing a cleavage like the Grand Canyon.

Hayley McLeod had been just behind them. She'd looked Robbie's way and giggled. Then, spotting a camera-toting Year 11, Hayley had stopped to pose like she was on the red carpet entering a film première.

Finally, and just as he was beginning to wonder whether Mel was going to get her own back by standing him up, she arrived. She looked great. Robbie leaped up, offered to buy her a drink, then shot off to the bar. While he was away, Hayley came out and hissed in Mel's ear.

'Sandra says it's all systems go! The kid with the camera will be hidden in the cookery room five minutes before the interval.'

'Does he know why?' asked Mel.

'Half-time entertainment,' said Hayley, 'with five quid in it for him if it all works out well. All you've got to do now is to get Robbie Brookes in there.'

'What about Malcolm Atwill?'

'Sandra says he'll be there if she has to carry him over her shoulder!'

Returning with two glasses – 'non-alcoholic, honest!' – Robbie suggested they hit the hall. Mel suggested they have a dance and they squeezed out onto the heaving dance floor. Above the DJ's head, noticed Robbie, the big screen was no longer blank. Shots were being flashed up, either from the overhead camera or from the roving version he'd seen Hayley pose for.

He caught the odd glimpse of the pair of them. Then a shot came up of Amazon Adams jiggling her low-cut self in front of a goggle-eyed Twilly, who seemed to be getting a lot more than the odd glimpse of another pair!

Twilly and Amazon were a lot closer when Robbie next spotted them on screen, some time later. Amazon appeared to have got Twilly in something resembling a bear-hug. What's more, she seemed to be overcoming the decibel level and was shouting something in his ear loudly enough for him to understand. He was nodding anyway, and looking smug.

Mel didn't have the same lung-power. As the interval drew near, she signalled that she wanted to go outside. *Fine by me*, thought Robbie. There was no other way he was going to be able to make any arrangements *Snogathon*-wise!

Mel took his hand and, feeling pretty smug himself, he allowed her to lead him out to a quiet seat in the foyer.

'I'm whacked!' she said, leaning back and closing her

eyes. 'I feel like going to sleep.'

Bad choice of words! thought Mel at once. A leery mention of bed could only be a breath away. But – no.

'You as well?' laughed Robbie. 'It must be me, I reckon. Mr Zyg's always dropping off when I'm with him.'

Mel opened her eyes again. 'The paper-shop man?'

'That's him.' Robbie nodded towards the packed hall. 'He'd have loved all this, would Mr Zyg. Dancing was his game.' He gave Mel a rueful little smile. 'Not any more, though. Mrs Zyg was talking about saving up for a good wheelchair the last time I was there.'

'He won't get better, then?'

'Mr Zyg? Nope. All he's fit for now is being read to.'

'Is that what you do, then? Read to him?'

Robbie laughed again, more brightly this time. 'Yeah. And you'll never guess what I read to him. Poetry!'

'You're joking!' said a disbelieving Mel, only to realise how wrong she'd been as Robbie gave a self-conscious nod.

'It's true. Wordsworth, Byron, Shelley, all that lot. Mr and Mrs Zyg both like poetry. It was Mrs Zyg who told me about that Shelley poem – y'know, the music one?'

'"Music, when soft voices die, vibrates in the memory",' said Mel without thinking. The poem that had turned Dave Carmichael round.

'That's it,' said Robbie. 'You should hear me, Mel. I near enough give Mr Zyg old Carmichael's lessons! Read him poems, tell him all about the things those dirty old poets got up to…'

He grinned, and Mel found herself laughing with him. 'They were a right bunch, weren't they?' she said.

'Yeah, well,' sighed Robbie. 'That's blokes for you.'

Then he realised that the foyer was starting to fill up a bit. The music had stopped and the walls weren't shaking. It was the interval – and so enjoyably had he been chatting that he'd completely forgotten about his big *Snogathon* plan. If he didn't act fast, he'd be too late.

'Mel…' he began, only to be interrupted by somebody else arriving at Mel's shoulder. Carmichael.

'I'm sorry to butt in, Miss Bradshaw, but could you spare me a minute?'

Mel looked up at him and said, 'Er…sure.' Getting to her feet, she glanced Robbie's way.

'See you back here, then?' he said.

'OK.' Mel made to follow Carmichael, only suddenly to turn back and murmur softly in Robbie's ear, 'Not here though. Somewhere quieter. I know. How about the cookery room? In ten minutes?'

Puffin' hell! thought Robbie, nodding his agreement faster than Noddy nodding hello to Big Ears, *I'm on to a winner and I didn't have to say a thing!*

Mel, too, had forgotten about the trap she was supposed to be setting up. Chatting to Robbie had been so…unexpected. So…nice.

But Carmichael's arrival had broken the spell. She'd switched back to Sandra's plan almost without thinking about it. Only as she followed the teacher up to his little corner in the English Department did Mel's conscience start to jab at her like a knitting needle between the ribs. She shrugged it off, occupying her mind with wondering what Dave Carmichael could want.

'I wanted to thank you, Miss Bradshaw,' said the teacher, as if he'd been reading her mind.

'What for?'

They'd reached his little corner. The *Wallace and Gromit* mug was back, now in pride of place slap-bang in the middle of his virtually bare desk. Beneath it was a sheet of paper.

'For this,' he said, sliding it free. 'Your coursework exercise. A poem about life and death. The Head gave it to me this afternoon. He said that it had had a major influence on the decision of the disciplinary panel.'

He held it out to Mel. 'As I say, I wanted to thank you for writing it.'

Mel took it. The title at the top of the page read, 'The Dancer'. But the name at the bottom said, 'Robbie Brookes.'

'I didn't write this, Mr Carmichael.'

The teacher smiled. 'I know whose name is at the bottom Miss Bradshaw, but – come on. You were his poetry partner. It's your work, isn't it?'

'No, it isn't. It's his. It's all his.'

The Dancer

He slumps in his chair,
Hardly moving at all.
His face is a blank,
Just like a brick wall.
His laugh is no more,
Nor his bellowing call.

He looks like a wreck,
To tell you the truth,
Except...to his wife.
Her eyes hold the proof
That she can still see
The dancer of her youth.

'Then...' said Carmichael slowly, 'I owe Mr Brookes an apology. I simply didn't believe that such a sensitive poem could be the work of...'

He didn't carry on. He didn't have to. Mel knew what he'd been going to say: *that a such a sensitive poem could be the work of a boy – particularly a boy like Robbie Brookes.*

A boy. A clown.

But – if a boy is ever going to realise it's no crime to be sensitive; if a clown is ever going to learn that it's not wrong to be thoughtful; if he's ever going to become sensitive enough and thoughtful enough to see a girl as a real person instead of a conquest...when does that happen? Had the process already begun for Robbie Brookes? And was she about to wreck it?

Burbling something to Dave Carmichael about having to go, she'd tell Robbie when she saw him, Mel ran.

Robbie watched the crowds pile out from the hall for the interval. Sandra Adams shouldered her way through a gap with a broad smile on her face and headed off in the direction of the loos.

Twilly, who'd been a few paces behind like the Duke of Edinburgh, turned in an entirely different direction. Hurrying across to Robbie, he hissed without breaking his step, 'Cookery room! Quick!'

The cookery room? For a quiet spot, thought Robbie, *that's going to be one puffin' crowded room!*

He turned to catch him. Too late. Twilly was already carving his way through the crowd like one of his precious racehorses racing through the field with the winning post in sight.

Robbie let him go, wondering if maybe it could just work out. Could he get down there, do his duty for Twilly, then be outside in time to meet Melanie? By then Twilly would be thinking his plan had worked and Sandra would have probably shot off home to find a powerful mouthwash. Twilly would be stuck. He'd have no chance for a second go and would just have to grind his teeth in anguish as he witnessed Robbie overtaking him with Mel!

Beginning to nudge his own way through the crowd, Robbie tried to imagine the sight that he was soon going to witness in that cookery room. Twilly and Amazon! If he wasn't careful, Twilly could get suffocated by that cleavage!

Puffin' hell, thought Robbie, *somebody the size of Mr Zyg could get lost in there, let alone a little squirt like Twilly!*

Mr Zyg…

Huge, powerful, gentle Mr Zyg.

Joking, bellowing Mr Zyg.

Loving Mr Zyg, always cuddling Mrs Zyg in their little storeroom.

A dancing, youthful Mr Zyg, light on his feet, spinning Mrs Zyg around to the sounds of music and laughter.

Mr Zyg, man enough to say he was sorry for talking

about Mrs Zyg as if she wasn't a person.

Mr Zyg – who wouldn't have had anything to do with this Snogathon *of ours*, saw Robbie as clearly as he'd ever seen anything.

The OM would. It would have been right up his street, because that was his style. And where had it got him? *What* had it got him? A wife who would walk out on him one day for sure. Not a woman like Mrs Zyg, who was going care for her man the way he'd always cared for her.

No, Mr Zyg wouldn't have touched the *Snogathon* because he'd have known, deep down, what Robbie had just tumbled to, what had been nagging at him for a while: that it wasn't right.

It just isn't puffin' right! That's what he was going to tell Twilly when he got to the cookery room.

Shouldering his way through the crowded foyer, Robbie had already left by the time Mel arrived. Sandra and Hayley swooped on her at once.

'Where have you been?' cried Hayley, wide-eyed. 'It's time!'

'I've changed my mind,' squawked Mel. 'Stop it, Sandra.'

'Stop it?' Sandra Adams snorted. 'Mel, it's unstoppable.'

'The roving camera kid went off before the interval,' giggled Hayley.

'And as for my little Malcolm,' cooed Sandra, 'he couldn't get down there fast enough once I'd suggested it.'

Mel looked round. The crowd was thinning. Dancers were drifting back into the hall for the second half of the disco. 'Robbie? Where's Robbie?'

Hayley's giggles reached a crescendo. 'Where do you think?'

'Melanie Bradshaw, we're proud of you,' said Sandra. 'Robbie Brookes was last seen walking briskly in the direction of the cookery room.'

After the din in the hall, the corridors leading round behind the stage area were like another world. Robbie's footsteps were echoing as he rounded the last corner. The door to the cookery room was down at the end. Robbie slowed, wondering how he was going to break the news.

Twilly wasn't going to like it. He'd probably come up with some instant rule that gave him Robbie's stake money. *Let him try*, he thought. He might just come up with an instant rule of his own, one that gave Twilly a poke in the eye.

'Robbie!'

He spun round. Mel was haring his way. And, behind her, rumbling along like a tank crossing Salisbury Plain, was Amazon Adams. Thankfully, Mel got to him first.

'Er...hi!' she cried. 'What are you...what were you...forget it! Let's go.'

Robbie wanted to go. He really did. But a very angry Amazon was blocking the way and clearly in no mood to let them slide along the corridor wall past her, even if there had been enough room.

'What are you doing!' she spat at Mel.

Mel gripped Robbie's arm. 'Removing my half of the arrangement. If you want to deal with your half, Sandra, that's up to you.'

Sandra turned on Robbie then, jabbing a finger in the direction of the cookery-room door. 'Is that weasel Atwill in there?' she growled.

'As far as I know...'

She said no more. Muttering something Robbie didn't understand, something about the third drawer down, Sandra powered past him. Within a couple of quick strides, she was at the cookery room door and swinging it open.

'Hello-o! Mal-colm? Sandra's here...'

As the cookery-room door closed, Robbie looked at Mel blankly. 'What's going on? And what's in the third drawer down?'

'What's going on, Robbie Brookes, is that we know all about the *Snogathon.*'

Robbie closed his eyes in anguish. The rules. She must

have read the rules before giving them back. He could say sorry from now to eternity and he wouldn't get out of this one. Slowly he opened his eyes again – to find Mel waiting not to punch him but to answer the second part of his question.

'And as for what's in the third drawer down,' she said, 'I can't be certain, but my money would be on a little kitchen utensil called a garlic crusher.'

Right on cue, Malcolm Atwill's searing cry of fear shot through the wall. 'Strike that,' winced Mel. 'I *am* certain.'

The agonised wailing grew louder and more piercing to be joined, at a far lower decibel level, by the rumble of laughter from the hall as the roving cameraman did his stuff.

Robbie didn't know what to say. All he could murmur, when Twilly finally fell silent, was, 'I don't suppose you'll believe me – but I came down here to tell Twilly it was all off.'

'It might well all be off where he's concerned,' said Mel. 'And I do believe you, Robbie.'

'I'm sorry…'

'Save it for later,' Mel said quickly. 'For now, just tell me this. What were you going to do with the prize money if you won?'

What could he say? 'I don't know. I hadn't thought about it.'

'Then let me make a suggestion,' said Melanie, nodding at the cookery-room door, 'now that your witness has arrived...'

Sandra Adams had shoved a whimpering Twilly out into the corridor. His eyes were streaming and he was walking like he'd just got off a horse.

'Give it to your Mrs Zyg,' said Mel. 'Tell her it's to put towards that wheelchair – for her dancer. Promise?'

Robbie was still in a daze.

'Promise!' repeated Mel.

'Sure. But why...?'

Men, thought Mel. *You really have to spell things out for them sometimes.*

Moments later, Robbie knew that he was in no position to argue. Partly because he really did think her suggestion was brilliant. But mostly because Melanie Bradshaw had suddenly and unexpectedly brought her soft lips into delightful contact with his.

Elephant one, elephant two, elephant three...

Ah, puffin' hell. Who was counting?

Tag

Michael Coleman

Pete and his friend, Motto, are into graffiti...at first the raids are just a bit of fun, but the buzz is addictive and soon they are pushed into a confrontation with a notorious graffiti gang, the Sun Crew...

Changing friendships, gang rivalry, inner conflicts and a roller-coaster ride of a plot make this a terrific, unputdownable read.

'Coleman skilfully handles the change in mood from hard-edged tension to sharp poignancy, when Pete finally acknowledges the anger he feels about his father's death.'
Books for Keeps

1 86039 654 2
£4.99

Weirdo's War

Michael Coleman

"You scared, Daniel?"

You scared? How many times have you said that to me, Tozer? Hundreds.

But this time, it's different. We're not at school. He isn't towering over me in some distant corner of the school grounds asking, "You scared, Weirdo?" He hasn't got me in a headlock with one of his powerful hands wrenching my arm up…

No. We're here trapped under the ground with no way out…

'Tense and psychological.'
The Times

Shortlisted for the *Carnegie Medal*

1 86039 812 X
£3.99

Little Soldier
Bernard Ashley

When Kaninda survives a brutal attack on his village in East Africa he joins the rebel army, where he's trained to carry weapons, and use them.

But aid workers take him to London where he fetches up in a comprehensive school. Clan and tribal conflicts are everywhere, and on the streets it's estate versus estate, urban tribe against urban tribe.

All Kaninda wants is to get back to his own war and take revenge on his enemies. But together with Laura Rose, the daughter of his new family, he is drawn into a dangerous local conflict that is spiralling out of control.

Shortlisted for the *Carnegie Medal* and the *Guardian Children's Book Award*

'A gripping and compassionate tale.'
TES

1 86039 879 0
£4.99

Tiger Without Teeth
Bernard Ashley

Hard Stew punched him in the mouth with a fist like a knuckleduster.

'I want that bike, son, and that little smack's just for starters.'

Hard Stew always gets what he wants, but he's not the only thing chasing Davey. There's also a secret – the sort that jumps up on you and is more frightening than a hundred Hard Stews. The sort you've got to stare in the face. If you've got the guts…

1 86039 605 4

£4.99

The Drop

Anthony Masters

Sean Dexter was hanging upside down, legs strapped to a beam... A message had been scrawled across his forehead in black felt-tipped pen and Sean knew what it was... I'VE BEEN DROPPED.

The Drop is the latest weapon in the war between the Geeks and the Sweats. But there's worse to come. Much worse. Someone's going to get The Big Drop. And they might not live to tell the tale.

1 84121 427 2

£4.99

Day of the Dead

Anthony Masters

It should have been an exciting holiday in California...
a rare chance for Alex to spend time with his
globetrotting father. But Alex's father has other things
to think about: a secret which involves black plastic
coffins in the back of his truck and a trip across the
border into Mexico – and he's not taking Alex.

But one way or another this is one trip Alex is
determined to go on... And it will be a trip he never
forgets!

'Anthony Masters is on his best edge-of-seat form'
TES

1 86039 657 7
£4.99

Horowitz Horror

Anthony Horowitz

Nine nasty stories to chill you to the bone.

It's a world where everything seems nice and normal to begin with. But the weird, the surprising and the truly terrifying are always lurking just out of sight. Like an ordinary-looking camera with secret, evil powers; a bus-ride home that turns into your worst nightmare, and a mysterious computer game that absolutely nobody would play...if they knew the rules!

Whatever you do, don't take this book to bed with you...

1 84121 455 8
£4.99

More Horowitz Horror

Anthony Horowitz

Eight sinister stories you'll wish you'd never read.

Look out of the window. See if you're alone. You never know what horror is lurking out there...

Eight nerve-tinglingly nightmarish stories to make your skin crawl and the blood freeze in your veins. Unmasking the strange, the macabre and the downright diabolical in everyday life these stories will make you think...they'll make you shiver...they'll make you afraid...

1 84121 607 0

£4.99

More Orchard Black Apples

☐ Weirdo's War	*Michael Coleman*	1 86039 812 X
	£3.99	
☐ Tag	*Michael Coleman*	1 86039 654 2
☐ Little Soldier	*Bernard Ashley*	1 86039 879 0
☐ Tiger Without Teeth	*Bernard Ashley*	1 86039 605 4
☐ The Drop	*Anthony Masters*	1 84121 427 2
☐ Day of the Dead	*Anthony Masters*	1 86039 657 7
☐ Horowitz Horror	*Anthony Horowitz*	1 84121 455 8
☐ More Horowitz Horror	*Anthony Horowitz*	1 84121 607 0
	£4.99	

Orchard Black Apples are available from all good bookshops,
or can be ordered direct from the publisher:
Orchard Books, PO BOX 29, Douglas IM99 1BQ
Credit card orders please telephone 01624 836000
or fax 01624 837033
or e-mail: bookshop@enterprise.net for details.

To order please quote title, author and ISBN
and your full name and address.
Cheques and postal orders should be made payable to 'Bookpost plc.'
Postage and packing is FREE within the UK
(overseas customers should add £1.00 per book).

Prices and availability are subject to change.